Fractious

By Debbie Graham

Order this book online at www.trafford.com/08-0143
or email orders@trafford.com

Most Trafford titles are also available at major online book retailers.

© Copyright 2008 Debbie Graham.
Cover design/Artwork by Alan Graham.
All rights reserved. No part of this publication may be reproduced, stored in a retrieval system, or transmitted, in any form or by any means, electronic, mechanical, photocopying, recording, or otherwise, without the written prior permission of the author.

Note for Librarians: A cataloguing record for this book is available from Library and Archives Canada at www.collectionscanada.ca/amicus/index-e.html

Printed in Victoria, BC, Canada.

ISBN: 978-1-4251-7026-4

We at Trafford believe that it is the responsibility of us all, as both individuals and corporations, to make choices that are environmentally and socially sound. You, in turn, are supporting this responsible conduct each time you purchase a Trafford book, or make use of our publishing services. To find out how you are helping, please visit www.trafford.com/responsiblepublishing.html

Our mission is to efficiently provide the world's finest, most comprehensive book publishing service, enabling every author to experience success. To find out how to publish your book, your way, and have it available worldwide, visit us online at www.trafford.com/10510

 www.trafford.com

North America & international
toll-free: 1 888 232 4444 (USA & Canada)
phone: 250 383 6864 ♦ fax: 250 383 6804 ♦ email: info@trafford.com

The United Kingdom & Europe
phone: +44 (0)1865 722 113 ♦ local rate: 0845 230 9601
facsimile: +44 (0)1865 722 868 ♦ email: info.uk@trafford.com

10 9 8 7 6 5 4 3 2

Always being an avid reader I studied English Literature and Language to A'level standard at college then embarked on constructive and creative writing courses as a hobby. I have had many short stories anecdotes and puzzles published across a range of media but always wanted to write a novel. This first novel forms the basis of a trilogy the second being almost complete and the third plotted.

    I lived in and around London for most of my life and worked as a Cardiac Technician for many years in a busy District General but moved to West Sussex with my Husband and dogs two years ago. Now working part time I have the opportunity to indulge my passion for writing and develop the career I have always wanted.

Prologue

The well aimed kick made him crumple to his knees the fire burning deep in his scrotum, the tears running down his cheeks and the bile rising in his throat. Linda Gerraty pulled the flick knife from her pocket and drew it across his throat with a steady hand before he even knew what had happened. As she watched the blood spurt from the wound and soak the front of his T- shirt the warm feeling of satisfaction spread through her stomach and made her smile. Linda Gerraty gave freebies to no one and this one had thought that he could get away with a quick blow job down a dark alley and walk away without giving her a penny because she was only a kid, but at thirteen Linda Gerraty may look like a little girl but her heart was far from pure. Raped, beaten and used by almost every man she had ever come into contact with since she was eight years old she had decided long ago that no one would ever use her again. She'd use what she'd got to make money and didn't care who she hurt along the way. Linda was sure this man had an unsuspecting little Wife at home maybe even a couple of kids but he needed to get sex and excitement somewhere else, well that was his problem but if he didn't want to pay for it, it was his own funeral and now he had met her that's exactly what it would be, his funeral. Linda stayed around long enough to watch him take his last breath that was the part she enjoyed most watching some bastard who had tried to cross her dispatched to another world by her own fair hand, he hadn't been the first and she knew full well he wouldn't be the last. Linda had always had to look after herself, she had followed in her Mothers footsteps and had always had to tom to survive but unlike her Mother she didn't intend to be found dead in a ditch at the side of the road killed by some dissatisfied customer or some tight bastard who didn't want to pay for his pleasure. Linda Gerraty had ambition and one day she was determined that her name would be known all over London and no one would dare to try and cross her again.

Chapter 1

He never asked me if I was married, honest he didn't, I don't really know what I'd have said if he had but he didn't, he didn't want to know. He wanted sex, plain simple sex, well actually now I come to think of it not that plain and simple but sex, he knew what he wanted and he knew how to get it. I'm not complaining the sex was fantastic, mind blowing but that was all it was sex, no forever, no commitment just a physical activity that I needed. I never imagined I could need that outpouring of energy but I did and I enjoyed every minute of it.

I met Toby through Pandora, Pandora my spiky, leggy mouthy best friend who also happens to be a decoy a paid honey trap who lures unsuspecting men into her web for their very suspecting, very jealous, very rich wives. Pan has everything deep green eyes you could loose yourself in, lean proud bone structure that makes those eyes even bigger and café au lait skin which means she needs very little make up to look absolutely stunning. A slick of lip gloss a dusting of rich brown blusher and she was set like Kate Jackson out of Charlie's Angels, the only difference being her hair no flowing locks for her she's very much you're wash and go girl. Short spiky henna red hair with the blackest tips makes her face look elfin and if she fancies a touch of sophistication she'll slip on a pair of totally useless clear glass spec's, guaranteed to catch the eye of any horny hooray Henry on the prowl for extra marital pursuits.

I've known Pandora since we were nine at school, all through Uni and work placements but whereas I went on to become a teacher she excelled at everything she tried. First she worked in a solicitors office as a lowly junior but it wasn't long before she had all the men falling at her feet and all the women sharpening their nails and sticking their husbands and boyfriends in chastity belts whenever they were within three hundred yards of her. She left when the senior partner's wife found out he had been taking pictures of her for his own exercise routine involving his right hand, he tried to explain he was in training for the county discus throwing competition but she didn't seem to think this was entirely true. Poor Old innocent Pandora looked like she was on her way out as Mrs. Rossiter seemed to think she shouldn't have posed for the pictures in the first place. Her attitude soon changed when Pan pointed out that good old Mr. Rossitor had written some promotional modelling work into her contract and she being young and innocent hadn't questioned it at the time when he had insisted she take her clothes off for him as he was an amateur photographer or why a solicitors office should need promotional pictures that would be better off in the pages of Escort or Razzle. The result goodbye Pandora with a huge settlement to keep her mouth shut and a full portfolio of stunning nude shots to put on her newly devised C.V.

With money in her back pocket and time on her hands she decided to pursue a new career this time as an agent in the modelling world using her own pictures to lure other models onto her books. She had no contacts, no experience but set out in true Pandora style to make it work and due to her determination succeeded. She called every publicity mogul, photographer magazine and fashion house she could find spending days at a time in the local library and on the internet making lists and deciding which contracts would be more profitable, she got knock back after knock back on the phone but as soon as she had persuaded an agent to see her, she was in, one look at her and another look at her own portfolio and he was smitten.
Gavin would demand business lunch after business lunch which then progressed to quiet meals in the evening and it wasn't long before Pandora was giving him close up's of his own and being rewarded with lucrative contracts for both herself and the other models that were flocking to join her agency as her fame grew.
Throughout this time she was learning her trade, sucking from him all his secrets, his contacts and all she needed to know about his wife and family and storing it all up for future reference, that's one thing about her she's not just a pretty face she has a mind like a steel trap and a ruthless streak as wide as the M25 when it comes to men.. In Pandora's mind men are on this earth to be used as stepping stones, sex toys

and to make her life a little easier she is totally heartless and never remorseful about her behaviour.

When it came, it hit poor Gavin like a bolt from the blue he was merrily meeting Pan at least three times a week, she's a master at blow jobs in unusual places and making him feel like a king, when they progressed to spending afternoons in luxurious hotel rooms he had no idea that whilst he was repaying the compliment as she insisted upon and fucking her to his heart's content she was also tipping off other competitors and treating them to the same carnal delights. It was only a matter of time before she indulged in a little pre arranged pillow talk and that rival oh, so stupidly let it slip to his wife that he was indulging in copious sex sessions whilst she was at home looking after the kids thankful for what she was getting in the sex department when he wasn't too tired after his heavy work schedule. he was devastated not only had he lost his family, he'd also lost most of his business and respect in the industry but funnily enough his real regret was that it was now over with Pandora

She had made him feel incredible, she'd encouraged him to indulge in all his fantasies, told him he was the biggest, the hardest the strongest she'd ever had, that he was the only one that could give her the earth shattering orgasms she experienced with him and he believed her. She was an excellent actress and all her men believed they were the biggest the hardest the strongest but there again they all believed that she had only ever slept with five men in her life so she was either a born again virgin or had a few tricks up her sleeve that none of us know about and it just goes to show how foolish men can be when their dicks are involved.

Pandora has always been strong willed and known what she wants and has never been afraid to do whatever is necessary to achieve her aims so when she decided to become a decoy I was worried but not shocked danger is in her blood a 9-5 existence would never suit her she'd be bored stiff she'd been looking for something exciting and unusual and she'd found it decoying. Decoying was the perfect job, it combined her love of humiliating men at the same time as indulging her passion for money but what the wives that employed her didn't know was that it also slaked her ferocious appetite for sex because Pandora's "hits" weren't innocent, she didn't get the evidence she needed and call a halt to proceedings she enjoyed what she was doing. I called her once and said

"Pan what are you doing tonight?"

"Fucking a client why?"

"Does his wife know?"

"Why should she?"

"Pandora she employs you and she has trusted you with her Husband!"

"So what? If she is stupid enough to pay someone like me to spy on a husband she can't trust, if she can't be bothered to be his whore in the bedroom why should I care. Besides he's one sexy bastard and I'm horny there isn't anyone else free tonight."

"You're unscrupulous."

"Good girls like you don't get anywhere Lou, safe job, safe marriage, safe mortgage, when was the last time you and Wayne fucked, ah I mean fucked properly not just lie next to each other and have a quick fumble, I mean a good hard fuck one that leaves you gasping for more?"

"Well, well" I stammered "o.k. mind your own business Pandora you do stretch our friendship sometimes, I don't ask you about your sex life you just enjoy telling anyone who'll listen so don't pry into mine. Me and Wayne are fine we don't need you poking your nose in!"

"I rest my case, you can't even remember don't be surprised Lou if he looks elsewhere, men like Wayne always do they need sex, not some little mouse sitting at home waiting to be asked, they need to be offered, to know it's available whenever they want it and know that you enjoy it don't make him feel that he's forcing you or that it's a chore you've got to make him think you can't wait to shag him on the kitchen table or blow him off in the park, worship his cock Louise otherwise you'll end up alone believe me!"

"When did you become such an expert on my husband? Is there something I should know?"

"Don't be childish Louise I wouldn't touch Wayne with a barge pole, not because he's unattractive because he bloody well is, but because he's your husband I'm just telling you to look after him because not every woman's got my principles and yes Louise I do have principles where friends are concerned" with that she slammed the phone down.

I know Pandora means well but I don't need advice like this I am acutely aware of my faults and horribly familiar with what I lack, I also know that next to Pandora I am very much the ugly duckling and have always wondered why Wayne chose me over her, I can't compete but with Wayne it has always seemed that I haven't needed to he has always appeared happy with his socially inadequate wife but when Pandora behaves like this I always end up feeling insecure and suspicious of everything he does. I am always telling myself who needs friends like her when she's in this mood and that I'd have a much quieter life without her but I love her, I always have done and when push comes to shove she's always been there for me.

Chapter 2

Pandora soon became bored with the modelling world and to tie her down is near on impossible so it was only a matter of time before she appointed a manager a bit of an enigma, a hugely intelligent man, late thirties, wiry, balding never wasted words unless he had to, abrupt to the point of rudeness at times and yet very sweet and caring once he knew and trusted you. Jeremy Watson had a certain presence when he walked into a room, he wasn't loud, didn't intentionally make an entrance and yet women and men alike seemed strangely drawn to him and fought to be in his company, Jeremy for his part looked uncomfortable among strangers and wouldn't have been out of place at any Nightclub door instead of being a respected and admired member of all the best and the worst clubs in London. Known by most, feared by many and yet feted by all who really knew him. The patience of Job was often needed to deal with Pandora let alone the girls she employed but Jez as he was known dealt with the tantrums, the traumas and the everyday running of the agency with sensitivity and discretion, all the girls knew he would help them out of any sticky situations whether it be with unwanted boyfriends or erratic finances and demanding landlords he would get them sorted and back on track with the minimum of fuss and in record time.

Jez worked like a Trojan for Pandora, kept his head down ran the agency with military precision profits were rising all the time and her clientele had increased threefold since Jez took over, other agents respected him and liked working with someone less complicated and emotional than Pandora., many of the men knew the stories about her and were loathed to work with her especially if their wives found out, too many people who became involved with Pan ended up divorced or in marital strife and the men in the modelling world had often avoided temptation too long to get caught out for the sake of a pretty face. Jez's life was his work, he seemed to have no past, no family, no ties and no commitments, he enjoyed what he did and kept whatever private life he had just that, private, he told no one anything that they did not need to know, either about himself or anyone else. He had become Pandora's rock in a very short space of time but his loyalty to her was unwavering, there was no sexual attraction, at least not for him he just respected her honesty and ruthlessness.

Business in safe hands Pan looked around for something else to occupy her time Never one to sit still too long she hit upon an idea to start a decoy agency. She would later tell me I was her inspiration because of my undoubting trust and loyalty to Wayne my husband, but I think the idea of sleeping around with other women's husbands and getting paid for it was her real reason for starting the service and her constant need to change the men in her life as well as in her bed. Sitting in her garden one sunny August day drinking long cool glasses of Pimms with half the salad counter of Harrods in she casually mentioned her plan for the future,

"Lou what do you think of a decoy agency?"

"A what, what's that then?"

"You know, women or men who pose as in the market for a pick up but are really employed by the partner."

"No Pan your not, you're not thinking of doing that!"

"Why not, other women do it don't they"

"It's too dangerous; please don't tell me you're serious"

"I am Lou, I need some excitement, I need a challenge it will be great spending other peoples money in bars and restaurants, meeting gorgeous men and setting up the chase, it's just what I need"

I looked around her beautiful garden, the manicured lawn, the Bougainvillea, Jasmine and Honeysuckle climbing the old stone walls, the pretty well stocked flower beds and the designer wrought iron furniture we were sitting on. Pandora had everything. The house was Georgian, situated in one of the most expensive areas in London, the view from her bedroom Hampstead Heath, her neighbours were a well known television duo who oozed smugness all over our TV screens whenever you could bring yourself to watch daytime telly and her maid earned more than I did in a year as a primary school teacher. Her house was stunning behind the severe exterior and high Georgian windows lay a treasure trove of delights. Every room was hung with originals by both old masters and modern contemporary artists, the walls painted in a delicate shade of pecan to compliment the high ceilings and original friezes her four bathrooms were tiled top to bottom with the finest Italian marble money could buy, everything was perfect her furniture bought from only the finest stores made to her own specification, the leather being flown over from Argentina and dyed in a warehouse on the outskirts of Essex to perfectly match her curtains and compliment her colour schemes. She was nothing if not a perfectionist and this showed in her home, my shoe boy on the outskirts of Heathrow would have fitted into her guest room but she was never happy, why had she always wanted more?

"Pan it's dangerous, you know that you can't just go around interfering in other people's lives because you want to, because it's your latest whim, families are important you can't keep making other people suffer because you had a hard upbringing what about the kids involved?"

"Louise stop getting all high and mighty, would you not want to know, would you want to bury your head in the sand and live a lie?"

"Were not talking about me and we're not talking about you doing the right thing crusading for wronged women if you were you wouldn't sleep with them and I know that's what will happen, you can't stop yourself. What does that leave these women with, a husband that's sleeping with two women instead of one and an empty bank account to boot!"

"I knew you wouldn't approve I knew you'd be jealous and want to pour cold water and scorn on my brilliant idea"

"Not so brilliant Pan it can only lead to disaster and heartbreak" Pandora turned her back and flounced off into the house, as she always did when she couldn't win an argument walk away, change the subject and ignore everyone else's point of view. She was basically selfish, uncaring and always right in her own mind, no one else mattered as long as she was happy.

Pandora's life had started so differently, she was born on a tough housing estate, as was I but whereas I had a safe happy childhood she was dragged up, pushed between her Mother and Father, used as a punch bag by her Brothers and thoroughly unhappy. At school her teachers would mock her because she craved attention, they didn't seem to see the need in her and instead taunted her with claims she was just like her brothers, would never make anything of herself and would be pregnant by the time she left school. Most of them hadn't taken the time to get to know Pandora, they did not realise that the more they knocked her the more she would fight against them and prove them wrong, she was determined to kick against them, she would not be broken by their lack of faith in her and her core of steel would ensure that they were all wrong. She had no intention of being a failure in anyone's eyes even people she couldn't give a shit about.

It was years later after a drunken night of truth or dare at University that she finally admitted that her Dad had made her life a living hell, he'd been sexually abusing her for years, coming into her room at night whilst her Mum was at work, encouraging his little girl to help him in the garage, even in the swimming pool on family holidays and day's out. She had tried to tell her Mum but she wasn't interested she was too busy with her own sordid little affairs that she flaunted in front of her husband and children. We would often go to her house after school to find a naked stranger walking around and it wasn't always men either, often it would be a woman that had taken Carry's fancy, she definitely believed in trying it all and male, female. Black white or yellow made no difference to her. These affairs were common knowledge and if my own Parents had known I had spent many after school hours around there instead of at my other friend Karen's they would have had a fit. I learned more about sex education listening to carry's afternoon antics than I ever did at school. When Pan had told me all those years later what had been going on with her Father there was no self pity, no bitterness, just the facts, that was that, chapter closed she couldn't change the past so just shut the chapter and move on.

    I couldn't argue with Pandora anymore, what was the point she will do what she feels is best for her and never thinks too far ahead, I had to give in to keep her friendship which I would rather have than her hatred and just pray that she would be safe and get bored with the idea before she had her first job, at least if we stayed friends I would know where she was and what she was doing whereas if we fell out I would have to sit and worry about her safety whenever she went out. This situation would test our friendship but what choice did I have.

    So she went ahead and started the agency and to hell with everyone else. It started really slowly which led me to believe or at least hope that it wouldn't be successful but then she was contacted by a very glamorous but older lady who suspected her husband had been having an affair with a girl in his office. Janelle Anstruthers was the type of woman Pandora could easily become. Very well groomed with shoulder length glossy blond hair and a bone structure that could support the fourth bridge, not only was she very rich she was also supremely confident and serene. In an uncharacteristic fit of self doubt Pandora had asked me along to this first meeting saying it would put my mind at rest as to the calibre of people she would be dealing with, but surprisingly I could see how nervous and self conscious she was, I had thought nothing unnerved her but this proved me wrong she was seriously rattled. Mrs. Anstruthers opened the door to her home which was little less than a scaled down version of Buckingham Palace but seriously tasteful and sophisticated, I couldn't imagine Janelle Anstruthers getting married sitting on a mock Tudor throne or parading the fact that her marriage was under strain to the Paparazzi she had too much class and poise. Janelle's home was like something out of house and gardens every inch beautiful every wall cool and contemporary and yet not cold or formidable the house looked lived in. creams and beiges complimented the highest quality solid oak floors, each room had tastefully coordinated curtains and furnishings all slightly varying with the next which gave the impression that each space had a very defined purpose and a use and personality of it's own, big houses are often impersonal and a little daunting but this one was homely and even the huge kitchen, which was a triumph to modern design still managed to maintain a welcome cottage feel to it. It contained every modern labour saving device but seemed that it wouldn't have been out of place in the Gloustershire countryside instead of the Surrey suburbs.

Janelle gave us the guided tour she was obviously very proud of her home and enjoyed showing it off which I could fully understand "I'm not a kept woman you know, I paid for this house" she informed us as she took us around the vast house and perfect gardens.

"I didn't imagine you were" Pandora said relaxing slightly

"Until I met my husband I was a very successful business woman." she didn't expand on what business she had been in and unusually neither of us asked which is against both of our nosey natures but something held us back from asking this woman too many questions she had an air about her that said my business is my own and after all she was Pandora's prospective employer.

"I worked hard for many years and Rory and I have only been married for 10, he is a little younger than me and didn't bring as much to the marriage, it didn't seem to matter though."

For the first time ever I heard Pandora speak to someone with near on respect when she asked tentatively:

"What does your husband do for a living Mrs. Anstruthers?"

"He dabbles Miss Green, unfortunately since marrying his drive to earn a living has diminished and he now lives off my money most of the time unless he stumbles across a lucrative investment, then it's pot luck as to whether he wins or loses my money, he's not what you would call a financial wizard."

"Don't you mind him doing that when it's your money" this was the old Pandora back insensitive, to the point and blatant.

"No money comes and goes, I've learnt that over the years but my husband I intend to keep. It took me a very long time to decide I wanted to marry and even longer to find the right man and although he has his faults, I can forgive them, he is rather a soul mate or I thought he was until this little lot reared it's ugly head."

We were sitting in the lounge overlooking the perfect greens of Wentworth golf course, the afternoon sun beating down on the retired overstuffed old men taking their daily exercise on the course.

"May I ask how you want our help" I questioned.

"I don't want your help Mrs Carter, I never ask for help, I want to employ you, and they are two very different things. I have friends, I also have enemies, I don't need to crowd my life with anyone else, what I want from you is a job of work nothing more nothing less, help does not come into it."

I was stunned into silence what had seemed a very pleasant woman had made it very clear as to what she thought of us and how Pandora would be treated whilst working for her and if I were her I would be ready to head for the hills, poor I may be but I do have a little self respect. Pandora on the other hand had noticed something of herself in Mrs. Anstruthers and although she later admitted she didn't much like what she saw she wasn't about to run away from a woman who she was so similar to.

"So what would you like us to do then Mrs. Anstruthers?"

"I want to find out just exactly what my husband get's up to in his spare time, I am perfectly aware that I have some years on him but whilst I am supporting him I have no intention of suffering his infidelities and once I have proof rather than suspicions I will deal with him."

I wasn't sure I like the way she said that but after our last exchange I decided to keep my mouth shut. We left soon afterwards and Pandora was bubbling with excitement. She had her first job and she couldn't wait to get started but I was more wary. I did not like Janelle Anstruthers one little bit and I felt uneasy about Pandora's prospects with her

It had been arranged that Pandora would be in Dusty's the local wine bar every evening for the next week armed with a picture of the very gorgeous Rory Anstruthers, she knew her target but as usual she'd set herself a little challenge which was to hook her prey on their first meeting. She had talked me into coming on this first assignment even though Wayne my husband was getting increasingly worried about my spending all my spare time with her. It didn't matter that I had been almost a football widow for the last three years since he had become interested in the game. Never one of her greatest fans Wayne was concerned that I was getting into a dubious venture with his greatest rival for my time and I don't think he liked the thought of his fellow man being duped into a confession by Pandora with my help. As usual Pandora looked drop dead gorgeous in a short powder blue leather mini skirt, cream knee length leather boots and cream lace top which left nothing to the imagination as the zip was undone enough to show off her assets and hint at what lay beneath. I was in my trusty well cut black trousers and a long silk burgundy blouse hoping not to stand out and to blend into the background, I had chosen the colour especially for this reason as it matched the wallpaper perfectly noticed our prey straight away and as usual all eyes turned to Pandora as we made our entrance. The women's eyes glazed over as they realised they had lost the attention of their male companions as they all surreptitiously turned to look at us and Pandora never one to shy away from attention likes to make all other women aware that if she so wished she can grab their male's attention whenever she enters a room and feels like being the centre of attention. We made our way to the bar and ordered our drinks, I'm sticking to mineral water but Pan orders a large glass of house red, as she gets her purse out to pay a cultured voice behind us says "let me pay for those it's my birthday"

We both giggled as this was the oldest chat up line in the book but our smiles are soon turned to astonishment when we realise that she's hit jackpot already, standing in front of us is no other than the truly enormous figure of Rory Anstruthers, tall, built like the proverbial brick shitehouse and with the smiliest brown eyes I had ever seen in my life. My heart sank as I knew that as soon as Pandora saw this Adonis that would be it, never one to keep her knickers on easily I knew they would be dangling from the lampshade before the night was out, she wouldn't be able to stop herself and this made my blood run cold at the same time as my groin tightening and flooding with wet juices of anticipation. He literally took my breath away but as I expected he was staring straight at Pandora and having a hard job even registering that I was there.

Chapter 3

Wayne was 22 when I met him 3 years older than me and devastatingly handsome in my eyes, he had an easy charm that made him popular with males and females alike and a sense of humour that could adapt to any situation he was in, he won fans wherever he went with his warmth and personality and as far as I could tell had never made any enemies along the way. The party was being held by a girl in our halls of residence, neither Pandora nor I actually knew her but with those parties you just turned up and as long as you bought a bottle no one cared who you were. At these do's the halls were just open house to everyone, all the room doors were flung open and most of the party was conducted in the corridor or on the stairs so often no one really knew who was having the party anyway.

Wayne stood out like a sore thumb from all the Uni Students; he looked clean for one thing, had a good haircut and fashionable well cut clothes. His whole attitude was in contrast to the rest of the people at the party you could tell immediately that he wasn't there just to get drunk he was pacing himself I don't think he would have been very proud of himself if he had thrown up all over the next guest that tried to hold a conversation with him as many of the students made a habit of doing and he didn't seem to be enjoying himself either. He was there because it was his sisters 18th birthday party and he felt obliged to attend. I wouldn't say he looked uncomfortable but he definitely didn't look as if this would be his chosen Saturday night venue and you got the feeling he was waiting for the opportunity to make a quick exit without letting his sister down and being the first to leave. When I first caught sight of him he had been backed into a corner by the college bike, a girl who's motto on life was have as much sex with as many men as possible before your twenty, just in case at that grand old age your fanny shrivelled up and you lost all feeling below the waist. I felt she was more in danger of having Euro tunnel approaching her and asking if they could hire her for their next route but she had her theories on life and was determined not to miss out on any man who had a pulse. Wayne looked like a mouse in a trap, eyes darting around the room trying to work out his escape route when our eyes met, he may as well have had a huge neon sign over his head flashing out help every few seconds, those big brown eyes pleading with me to set him free from her clutches. At first the sadistic streak in me left him to suffer, I smiled across at him and carried on talking to the group I was with from my own year but I couldn't resist keep glancing over to where he was and at last I couldn't hold out anymore, he looked so vulnerable and upset I took a slow walk over, holding his gaze in mine all the time so that he knew I would be his saviour and he wouldn't have to suffer much longer.

Much to the bikes annoyance as soon as I arrived on the scene Wayne angled his body away from her and her constant chatter and managed to remove her hand from it's proprietarily place on his arm, he started to talk as if we had known each other for years instead of being complete strangers

"Hi there how are you haven't seen you for ages"

"I'm fine thanks I replied how about you?" I asked trying not to laugh at his strained pleading

'Great, I was wondering how your Mum was and that sister of yours; I haven't seen her for years!"

I had to give him points for winging it, I actually don't have a sister but luckily Miss Chopper 1999 doesn't know me well enough to know that and I had always been careful to keep my somewhat over active brothers out of her reach, I had never fancied her as a sister-in-law and the boys seemed to have a penchant for shall we say women that's knickers where not only held up by elastic but should have been on braces for easy access, the problem was they also used to forget themselves now and again and had come very close to shot gun weddings before and this was one girl I'd rather use the shotgun on myself than have to admit she was one of the family.

"Which sister do you mean?" I replied and watched the horror cross his face as he frantically searched around for a name, as he didn't yet know mine he was smart enough to realise he could be treading on a minefield. I enjoyed watching him grope around for a while, begging me with his eyes to give him a clue, it was nice watching him sweat and that vulnerable look come back again but in the end I had to put him out of his misery,

"Do you mean Claire or Nicole?" I could almost hear the sigh of relief escape his lips as his face lit up with a smile believing he had been saved from further humiliation and seeing me as the solution to his limpet problem,

"Nicole of course, I used to see her a lot but it must be years now"

"Oh I thought it was only about 18 months, Harry's only 9 months old so it can't be anymore than that, although we wouldn't expect you to remember that as you've not seen him since he was born!" his complexion changed from a healthy sun kissed tan to the colour of the White Cliffs of Dover in a matter of seconds, he was just lost for words and looked like he might be sick, he had thought he was out of the woods and had managed to avoid a nasty public scene with the limpet when he tried to disentangle himself from her clutches but he now realised he was in danger of looking an even bigger shit than if he had just told her to "piss off." Five or six heads swivelled round and people seemed to close in to get a better look at the man who had never even bothered to see his child, he looked cornered and his colour was now flushed and on a par with a pillar box. "I had nothing to do with that" he spluttered

"Well that's not what Nicole said, heartbroken she was and it hasn't been easy for her, Harry's an awful baby, must be like his Father, selfish and always wants his own way!"

"Hold on a minute I never even slept with your sister"

"I knew you were a shit but I never thought you'd sink that low to deny your own Son!"

"Please, please," He suddenly realised he didn't even know my name yet but almost everyone else in the room would so to make one up and take a chance would be social suicide and he was desperate not to keep digging the whacking great hole he was in danger of falling in. I had to give in, I couldn't put him through anymore, I had thought he would have a greater ability to bluff himself out of any situation but I had judged him wrong, I started backtracking. I had heard someone earlier mention his name was Wayne so I had an advantage on him "Michael Cosgrove I don't know how you can stand there and lie like that!"

"No, no I'm not Michael Cosgrove, I have never heard of Michael Cosgrove I'm Wayne, Wayne Carter I thought you had the wrong person I haven't seen Nicole for at least four years could be more" I could see he could have cried with relief and gratitude even though it was me that had put him in that situation in the first place but I realised Wayne had a soft side and didn't like people to think badly of him. I continued with the farce,

"Oh, oh I am so sorry I was sure you were Harry's Dad, I feel such a fool" I think he could have kissed me but it had achieved the aim I set out to meet, getting rid of the bike. She and the other earwiggers had lost interest when they realised that the stranger didn't have a murky past and there wasn't going to be a fight equal to the gunfight at the O.K corral. At that point I realised how stupid I'd been, I didn't know this man and for all I knew he might have been a mass murderer or have the temper of an Irish navvy after fifteen pints but I needn't have worried, all of a sudden the corners of Wayne's eyes crinkled with laughter lines and he couldn't stop smiling.

"I'm sorry I didn't think, I'm good at that the mouth works before the brain, I didn't mean to make you so uncomfortable I just got carried away, I bet you wish I hadn't bothered to butt in and try to save you from the adorable Bianca's clutches now?"

"No I appreciated your help, I just wish you had thought of something more flattering than an absentee Father, a male model you'd seen in a Vogue magazine or a little known but hugely intelligent intellectual would have been more to my liking"

"In your dreams, don't believe in yourself too much do you? What do you actually do, or are you really undercover for M15 working undercover for James Bond?"

"Oh ha, ha no actually I'm a Carpenter, I work for myself making bespoke furniture, kitchens, bedrooms stuff like that, all very boring really but I enjoy it. You're a student here are you?"

"Yes not for long though I have my first practice post in a primary school next year, when I've finished that I'll be a qualified teacher under supervision so no longer the lay about student living off the state and enjoying the life of Riley I'm afraid"

"No just lovely long holidays and spending all day playing dress up and Mummies and Daddies whilst getting paid well for it"

I was going to launch into my spiel about teaching being a hard profession in this day and age but then I realised he was only winding me up and getting his own back and I couldn't blame him but I wasn't going to bite his snide remarks, I wanted to disappoint him and make him realise I'd won on points.

"That's right, envious?"

"Definitely" he knew when he'd lost and to cut his losses and run, I wasn't going to take the bait and play his game; I'd enjoyed my own too much. "good job if you can stand the kids, it's not been so long since I was one myself, so I can still remember what they get up to, I couldn't work with them all that noise would drive me mad"

"You get used to it, besides who are you trying to kid one yourself not so long ago, with those grey hairs I could have called you a Granddad rather than just a runaway Dad"

"Grey hairs are distinguished I'm quite proud of them and for you information I'm 26, not ancient even though I admit I look a bit lived in." I had to laugh at that he didn't look lived in at all in my opinion just very sexy and his hair added to that attraction but I wasn't about to tell him that.

"Are you enjoying yourself?"

"Talking to you, yes, the party, no not really all too Uni to me, I got passed the angry teenager stage, grew out of the Goths and got bored with the ten pints a nighter's so I'm always a bit lost at these do's"

"Want to go somewhere else?"

"Love to but I came with my friend Pandora and I'm not sure she would appreciate being dumped, let me see if I can find her and see what she's up to"

"Bring her along if you like" he must have seen my jaw drop as he added "I mean if you have to, it's not what I'd like but if you can't leave her I'm trying to show I can be a gentleman when required"

"O.K I'll be back in a minute"

I went in search of Pandora all the time hoping against hope that she wouldn't want to tag along as much as I love her she has always been my major enemy in the male stakes one look at her and my date disappears or spends the whole night talking to her or about her and I liked Wayne Carter, I liked him a lot and I didn't want to share him with Pandora until I'd had the chance to spend time with him myself. I wanted to enjoy his company a little longer before he decided he'd got the rough end of the stick and could have her instead

`I found her as usual surrounded by a crowd of admiring men, drooling over her every word and making her feel like she was the most interesting woman in the world, Carol Vorderman was a dunce in their eyes once Pandora started philosophising and flashing her smile. I don't suppose it helped that she was wearing a skirt that was little more than a belt sitting on the kitchen counter swinging her endless legs back and forwards rhythmically catching the eye of every male within 50 yards. As usual she was talking about her self and her view of the world which was all rubbish but from the rapt attention of her audience you would think she was the next candidate for Maggie Thatcher's job. Seemingly highly intelligent men become transfixed by Pandora, her combination of fuck me clothes, innocent pixie face and legs that go on for ever have every man she comes into contact with imagining what she could do to their nether regions and how those legs would feel wrapped round their necks in the throes of passion. I caught her eye as she was just about to perform her party trick of putting her leg round the back of her head which although vulgar had the desired effect of raising every males blood pressure and firing their imagination in the near vicinity especially as her choice in underwear was minimal and left nothing to the imagination. She saw me approaching and beamed giving a cheeky wink indicating she was pleased with the amount of attention she was receiving, I gestured that I was about to leave and was that O.K with her she mouthed back that would be fine as she lifted her leg above her head, I heard an almost orgasmic collective sigh from her ever growing band of followers as they were having their own private thoughts and dreams and made my exit quickly, the last thing I wanted was Wayne to follow me and see what my friend was doing, possibly because I did not want him to make a judgement on me by association but mostly because I did not want him to become mesmerised by her display.

Wayne was waiting by the door when I got back looking to make as quick a getaway as possible so I grabbed my coat and we were out the door like two spitfires

"Right any preferences?" he asked

"No as long as it's not another student party, what about your sister, will she mind you running out like this?"

No she's fine she didn't actually think I'd turn up so she's happy that I stayed for a while, she knew it wasn't really my kind of thing but we are close and I wanted to show my face and make sure she was enjoying herself"

"She's lucky to have such a supportive brother!"

"A rock that's me and ever so modest to go with it. How about something to eat we could go to the Napoli in West Street or if you fancy it the wine bar does good bar food, it's up to you, what do you like?"

"How hungry are you? I'm not too bad I wouldn't mind getting some French bread cheese and a bottle of wine, we could go and sit on the beach and talk properly without all the noise, but if that's not what you were thinking of that's fine, you choose" sounds good to me. I like a woman who's cheap"

"Don't you believe it I never said how much the wine was going to cost and as for cheap I assume you mean my taste in food because that's the only cheap thing about me!"

The local Deli was open until 11 so we popped in and bought a lovely fresh French stick, Brie and Borsin, some grapes and strawberries and a bottle spicy red Rioja, a rich liver pate laced with black peppercorns and some plum vine tomatoes finished our shop off. Next door the newsagent provided us with the plastic plates, cutlery and glasses we required and we headed off with our haul to the beach to sit among the beautiful golden sand dunes and eat our feast.

The evening was clear and bright and the breeze was building but not enough to be a nuisance, we sat looking out to sea, its vast expanse like a sheet of glass the odd ripple reminding us that it had a huge potential for danger as it glinted like a knife edge in the setting sun. I have always thought of the sea as a deadly entity at times so calm and welcoming enveloping you in its warmth and rhythmic movement yet other times its black depths pulling you down, sucking the breath from your lungs dragging you with it's current to its evil core never to return. We talked about everything ourselves, our families, our hopes for the future and what we wanted and expected from life. I quickly realised that I very much liked this man he was intelligent, sensible and yet fun at the same time, he talked about his family with true affection and despite his earlier comments on children which were made to make me rise to the bait he truly loved his young nephews and nieces, he had a very tender soft heart but at the same time where his business was concerned astute acumen and a sense of fairness and loyalty. I told him about my family that I'd always wanted to be a Teacher that I hated being away from home although I loved living by the sea and that I disliked intensely living in the halls of residence. I craved a home of my own and that was my first priority as soon as I was able to earn a proper wage. I also dared to tell him about Pan and our friendship although I missed out the bit about her being absolutely stunning and that I dreamed of having her self belief and confidence.

We sat talking until the sky was inky black and the stars twinkling, the wine finished and the hungry seagulls gorging on the remains of our supper, neither of us wanted to move but we knew it was about time we did, the air was now cold and the wind was whipping the sand into our faces. Wayne made the first move he pulled me onto my feet and kissed me deeply, urgently his tongue probing my mouth, his strong hands splayed along my back, I didn't want him to stop, I wanted this to go on forever. When he finally came up for air he hugged me to his chest so tightly I could hardly breathe

"Come home with me he asked?" Wayne shared a flat with a friend in a little village called Newton Poppleford over by Sidmouth, I desperately wanted to go home with him and spend the night in his bed but I knew I mustn't. I liked this man and I wanted to keep him, the way to do that wasn't to jump into bed with him on our first date I wanted to see how things developed before going too far.

"No Wayne I can't, I want to but I can't, I like you too much and I don't want a one night stand"

"I like you too Lou and I understand really I do I'm disappointed but I'm sure I'll live. I'd like to see you again though?"

"I'd like that too"

"How about tomorrow, I'll bring my car and pick you up about 10 we could go over to Budleigh walk along the cliffs to Ladram Bay, stop at the pub in Otterton and have lunch and see the floral displays at Connaught Gardens in Sidmouth. You'll love it, the smell and the colour are amazing from there you can go down onto the beach at Jacobs Ladder and we could have a swim"

"It sounds fantastic but are you sure you want to be saddled with me for another day you've already spent a whole evening talking to me when you could have been having fun at a party?"

"I'm having a good time Lou, I don't like parties and I've really enjoyed myself tonight more than I have in a long time"

"I have too; I'd love to come tomorrow. Thank you." We parted back at the halls after another long lingering kiss. I didn't sleep that night for dreaming about what it would be like sleeping with Wayne but I tried to concentrate on the evening we had spent together instead of the things I would like to do with him in the future.

Chapter 4

We spent the next day doing all the things Wayne said we would do, the weather was warm and sunny and we walked for miles ending up at Jacobs Ladder on the beach with some cold beers and fish and chips. The day went so quickly we were both shocked to realise it was 7 o'clock and we were hungry again even though we had a lovely lunch in the Black Horse Inn earlier in the day. We were both very aware it would almost be time to go home and I had already made up my mind that I didn't want to go home tonight, I had admitted to myself that if he didn't ask me to stay again I would be gutted and it would have spoilt the whole day, but I shouldn't have worried he did ask again and we headed straight back to his flat. Danny his flatmate was out for the night But Wayne said he was hardly ever there anyway spending most of his time with his girlfriend or working odd hours as a Chef, he said they could spend whole weeks without actually bumping into each other as Wayne worked for himself and often worked late into the night at his workshop so they would communicate through notes and e-mails, they got on really well when they did meet up and would go for a beer or stay in watching football but those times where few and far between.

The flat was very masculine but very neat and tidy, big furniture, most of it Wayne had actually made himself, wooden floors, clean lines no frills just plain and functional. Predictably the lounge was dominated by a 42 inch plasma screen TV and there being little in the way of ornaments apart from wooden carvings, no bric a brac or dust collectors which I like, I always think they make a room look cluttered and messy. But I didn't have too long to wander around, we were both too interested in getting to the bedroom so we went almost immediately along the hall to Wayne's room right at the end. The room was huge much bigger than I'd expected and the views over the Devon countryside were breathtaking, he even had a little balcony, which had always been my dream to have, I could see myself sitting out there in the mornings eating breakfast in the warm summer sunshine or spending evenings with a glass of wine watching the sun go down in the West, but it was becoming pretty obvious that Wayne was more interested in giving me a guided tour of his crotch than his flat so we made our way over to the bed.

He was already busy taking his shirt off at the same time as his tongue exploring my mouth and pushing my hand towards his restricted cock, his hands making their own tour of my breasts his breathing becoming more rapid and uneven. He'd pushed my bra up and was rolling my nipple between his long skilful fingers making them erect and engorged with blood, my breathing had become identical to his, the blood pumping through my veins like the formula one cars at Silverstone,

I thought if I didn't get him inside me soon I'd explode. I was busy rubbing my hand up and down the shaft of his not insubstantial manhood, stopping only to gently squeeze his balls and feel them contract with anticipation. At last we had finally managed to shed all our clothes and were laying on the massive bed that he told me later he had made himself, painstakingly carving all the detail and lovingly making sure all the joints fitted together perfectly without the need for glue or screws and taking months to ensure it was perfect in every way. He began to make his way down to my navel with hot wet kisses that felt like hot wax dripping onto my skin and enflaming every inch that his lips touched sending sparks of pleasure and pain straight to my groin making me writhe with the need to be filled my him at the same time as enjoying the wait and anticipation. He'd slowed down now taking his time, making sure I enjoyed the first time we had been together, he had no intention of rushing and was taking pleasure in the fact he was taking me to a place of passionate suspension and heavenly anticipation.

I continued to fumble around but the further he moved down my body the harder I was finding it to keep contact with his own erogenous zones, I mumbled at him to move around so that I could give him as much pleasure as he was giving me and he turned around so that he was suspended above me taking the weight on his elbows and knees and leaving me to admire his magnificent cock properly for the first time. I was now in a position to watch as I worked him, his foreskin moving back and forward allowing me to see the true length and thickness of him and causing small drops of pre-come to slide over his throbbing penis head making me want to lean over and taste its sweetness and lick its purple pulsating head

Wayne had hit his target and his tongue was flicking over my clitoris, down the inside of each labia and darting in and out of my waiting entrance, my body giving involuntary shudders letting him know that he was taking me to the point of no return, but pulling back and causing me to arch my back letting him know I needed more and making sure I knew he was fully in control and his intention to be the one to decide when it ended. I needed him to be inside me needed to feel his hardness, needed to wrap myself around his length, feel his balls squeezed up against my perineum have his pelvic bone pressing against my abdomen, I begged him to stop, to give me what I needed but he continued to work his magic with his tongue. It was no good I could not wait any longer all of a sudden a huge wave swept through my body I ground my crutch into his face wrapping my legs around his shoulders moaning although I was desperately trying to hold on to some dignity letting myself go as my orgasm ripped through my body and made me shudder uncontrollably, but he wouldn't stop, he continued to us his tongue and make me keep coming and coming until I thought I couldn't take anymore I had never felt anything like it before.

He emerged from between my legs, red, dishevelled but grinning all over his face pleased that he had achieved what he had set out to do and knowing he now had the upper hand, he sat back on his heels and said "I don't think I need to ask if you enjoyed that!"

I must have looked a bit embarrassed at my sluttish behaviour because he said there was nothing to be embarrassed about and that he hadn't finished with me yet.

I felt it was now my turn to return the favour and moved forward onto his erect dick moving my mouth slowly enjoying it's taste and smell, he lay back on the pillows, closing his eyes to fully enjoy the sensation as I took as much of him into my mouth as I could manage and doing my best to please him as best I knew how. I wasn't exactly very experienced in this area but I felt I needed to try to give him as much as he had given me I'm sure he had better but he wasn't exactly complaining as he lay there smiling gently and talking to me in a low seductive voice. We continued like this until I had to give up, my throat was sore and I desperately needed a drink but still I had not managed to make him come, just the odd dribble and he'd hold back again, his self control was superhuman. I had to concede defeat, I sat up and looked at him but he seemed to be meditating on some higher plane, that was obviously how he held back and kept in control, he suddenly opened his eyes and gave me a long lingering look "Finished?" he asked.

"For now, I have to admit I could really do with a drink" I replied

"Well I've never had that effect before, driving you to drink wasn't my intention, was I really that bad!"

"No not at all' I laughed 'Water will do but I just really need a drink."

"No chance of that we need a beer to keep us going for next time." he jumped off he bed and padded off towards the kitchen without a stitch on, I hoped his flatmate hadn't come home and heard us, I wasn't exactly quiet and now I was embarrassed, I'd made more noise tonight than I ever had before Wayne had just taken me to places I had never been and I had seemed to lose all my inhibitions and shyness, I'd never enjoyed sex so much and never had anyone to do the things that Wayne had just done. Mind you at the back of my mind I did wonder how many women he'd slept with to know so much about our bodies and our needs. He possessed an earthy quality that had made all this seem natural and romantic rather than seedy even though we had only just met.

When he came back we sat around talking and drinking our beers trying to recover our strength. I learnt that Wayne only had the one sister, they had been brought up in Exeter and had lived there all their lives, and other than the odd day trip to London when he was young he had never really travelled at all as a child. This was what spurred him on to take a year out and travel around Europe before coming back to start his course to become a master carpenter, he had always known that this was what he wanted to do as he had always had a love of all things wooden but he knew he had to travel a bit and see life outside Devon before he settled down to start his apprenticeship.

Wayne left home at sixteen and never went back to live. He got on great with his Dad and still tried to spend as much time with him as possible but his Mum was a different kettle of fish. He said he couldn't really give a reason why they didn't get on, that he couldn't really put his finger on what the problem was but that they were too different. He also felt she had a lot of secrets and was never 100% honest with people she always held too much back, Wayne felt honesty within a family was very important and because of this he always had this nagging doubt about his Mother which made their relationship an uneasy one. he came back to Devon because he loved it, he loved the Sea, the Countryside and the Animals and the feeling of space and calm it gave him. He couldn't see himself living anywhere else, he was happy here and although he had been to many different countries now he still knew this was where he belonged.

I told him about my Parents Brothers and how I missed London, the people, the shops and all the noise and how I couldn't wait to qualify and go back to work in a London school. I also bit the bullet and told him about my best friend Pandora. He was honest, he admitted that he had noticed her the night we met at the party which was a relief, I wouldn't have trusted a man who feigned ignorance about her presence, he also commented on her beauty but said she wasn't his type. The way she attracted men like bees around a honey pot and loved the attention she was getting turned him off, he said she was too obvious and brash for his liking.

That was the start of it all, we sort of started living together, not officially but bit by bit I began to move in my stuff and although I kept my room at the college we were never apart at night. We relaxed into an easy way of living together, we shared the cooking, shopping, the housework, we never spoke about these jobs we just seemed to match each other and respected each other enough to enjoy making our home together and sharing the work. The only cloud on the horizon was the knowledge that if or when I qualified I would have to go back to London. I had already applied and been accepted at a school in Ealing West London and I didn't feel that I could cause problems and drop out in my first year as a probationer, it would have been noted on my records and I may have gained a reputation for being unreliable which was the last thing I needed. I couldn't envisage Wayne leaving his beloved Devon but we didn't talk about it and just waited until after my exams to finally discuss the matter. To my surprise Wayne had already decided that he didn't want us to break up or to have to live apart so he was going to move with me, not forever he couldn't promise that but at least for a couple of years until I was established and out of probation and we could move back to the west country.

We married before we left to both of our families delight, not a big wedding because that wouldn't have suited either of us but a lovely day just how we wanted it without anyone else's intervention, we arranged it all ourselves so it was perfect for us. The house we started to buy was an investment, we didn't want to rent as Wayne wanted to make his own mark on our first real property together, we were assured the house prices in London where set to soar so we thought in the future we could sell it for a profit and return to set Wayne up in his own business again, he had taken a job at Heathrow airport as a baggage handler, he hated it but he knew it wasn't forever. We found a house that was small but close to both our works and as much as we could afford at the time. Neither of us was exactly happy living there but it was a means to an end and we were determined to make it work and stick it out.

Wayne made the house beautiful, it was small and didn't have a lot of room for all our things but he made all the furniture and spent all his spare time in the garden. We made friends and got on with all our neighbours we even bought a couple of dogs which was something we had both always wanted and now we had a garden we felt we could have and in the future when we went back to Devon they would have all the fields to run in they could wish for.

At around the same time Pandora had gone to work for Mr. Rossiter the Solicitor and come into her ill gotten gains. She called one day and asked if she could come and stay for a few weeks while she looked for a place to buy in London. Wayne wasn't exactly over the moon but he agreed to it in the end because he knew that I valued my friendship with her and wanted to make me happy. He was not best pleased when he would come down to breakfast and find a complete stranger raiding the fridge, walking around in a towel and using the hot water but he held his tongue and only whinged to me when Pandora was out of earshot. He wasn't one for confrontation or to cause problems but I know he was coming to the end of his tether when Pandora finally left. She only stayed for a couple of months but I am sure that is all his natural calm and good nature could have taken. I felt guilty but I never really felt good about Wayne and Pan being alone in the house together when he was off shift and I was at work, I trusted him but Pandora was a do now and think later kind of girl and I worried that in my absence passion might spark between them at anytime. It was a situation I didn't want to ponder on, to loose Wayne would be loss enough but to loose him to Pandora would be devastating.

Once she had gone our lives settled back down to normal, with no piles of knickers left laying around the house, no dirty dishes in the sink and best of all no feral noises of passion coming from the spare room on a nightly basis we went back to our settled some might say boring lives, but we were happy or as happy as we could be living in London.

Chapter 5

Having made her impression on Rory Anstruthers Pandora set about gaining her evidence and having her fun in her very own way. At that first meeting she made sure she had made him very aware of her sexiness and earthy humour and left him drooling for more and an ambition to get her into bed. Unlike her usual self Pandora didn't go in for the kill straight away and allowed Rory to woo her a bit before she let him into her bed, but when she did she achieved her aim to get him to fall for her hook, line and sinker.

Their first night was spent in the wine bar with them just enjoying each others company and talking and laughing together, I had disappeared back to my anxious husband as soon as I had assessed that Pandora was in no danger and Rory was not actually a sex starved mass murder, but a very nice man. I rang Pan next morning expecting all the gory details of her night of passion and was quite shocked to hear that they had talked for hours, even going back to her house but that after coffee she had sent him packing and spent a blissful night of sweet dreams anticipating their next meeting and having filthy thoughts of what would most definitely happen next. Rory had gained countless brownie points by telling her he was married and not trying to pretend his wife didn't understand him. What he had said was his marriage was unhappy because he wanted a family; he had made a mistake marrying Janelle because she was so much older and had never been the maternal type. He admitted that his head had been turned by her money, her glamour and her very notorious reputation in London's underworld, when I asked Pandora with some very uneasy feelings stirring in my stomach what that reputation was for she said she hadn't manage to find out yet but that Rory had made it sound very sinister. Before we hung up I begged Pandora to be careful and to stop seeing Rory, make her report to Janelle and cut and run, to think herself lucky that she hadn't slept with him and to get out before she was in too deep, but she refused. Pandora had no sense of danger and didn't like to admit defeat. Rory was obviously very smitten with her as he had insisted they meet again that day and Pandora had already arranged a hotel room to use for the afternoon.

    I put down the phone and sat at the kitchen counter feeling totally desolate, I felt worse than I had ever felt in my life and I had the feeling that something terrible would happen if she continued to carry on decoying if not with Rory then with someone else's husband. Pandora was not cut out for that type of work although she was well able to keep her feelings at bay she was not able to maintain a professional stance and keep her knickers on even if the husband was short, fat and bald. She liked all men she couldn't help it and she loved sex even more, that was something she had inherited from her Mother although I was never aware of her going with another woman, more than one man at a time but I think she drew the line at lesbianism. She seemed to have no conscience I was sure Rory would be highly delighted that she had taken the initiative to book a room and would be even more delighted to spend the afternoon with the gorgeous Pandora but would she still make her report to his wife? Pandora had taken a large wadge of cash from Janelle up front, she would never be able to hand it straight back even if it had crossed her mind to because Janelle would realise something was wrong and who knew what the consequences could be if she found out that Pandora had been adding to her problems by screwing her husband

Pandora had arranged to meet Rory at 3.30 in the bar of the Carlton Hyatt in Knightsbridge, she had booked the room in my name which I wasn't best pleased about but she didn't tell me until it was all booked and done and dusted so I couldn't really complain, she would only go into a sulk and refuse to talk to me and then I would have no idea if she was safe or not if she didn't call me later to let me know she was o.k but she couldn't see why I was so angry anyway so I just dropped the subject and let her get on with it..Pandora could be very mean spirited when she wanted to be and she thought it was hilarious to book the room in my name because she said it was something I would never have had the courage to do and she could never imagine me spending an illicit afternoon in an hotel room with a secret lover so she would do it in my name for me.

She arrived at the hotel early to set the scene for her seduction, candles, incence soft lighting and a beautiful cream silk negligee that left absolutely nothing to the imagination already in the room before she went back down to the bar to meet him although she told me later she had wasted her time because no seduction had been necessary. Rory had arrived ready for action, as soon as he walked into the bar and ordered another drink each he suggested that they get a room. He said he had not been able to stop thinking about her and that he wanted to take her to bed immediatley, Pandora gave her best shy demur smile and admitted to him that she had already booked one as she wanted him as much as he wanted her. Before the drinks could arrive he had taken her by the hand and they had disappeared into the lift. It was lucky there were other people in the lift otherwise she said they would have ended up doing it there and then. By the time they had finally got through the door Rory already had his trousers unzipped and his massive cock was showing just how ready he was, Pandora couldn't keep her hands off it and couldn't wait to get it inside her. Once the door had shut behind them all his pent up passion took over and he pushed Pandora back against the wall ripping her £40 a pair incognito wisp of white lace knickers aside and entering her without any preamble they were both so swept away with the attraction and passion they both felt. Whilst he pumped away at her and Pandora wrapped her legs around his waist willing him to thrust deeper and harder he kept up a constant stream of deeply offensive banter as if realising that this was what Pandora enjoyed, hard rough filthy sex, he seemed to have her weighed up and seemed only too pleased to oblige. His strong big hands cupping both her buttocks and squeezing them with every thrust Pandora's breath was taken away, not an easy feat to achieve with a girl of her experience she was having trouble holding on to her orgasm and when Rory moved his hand across so she was supported by it and bought the other one round to rub her clitoris she exploded immediatley holding on to him for dear life and squeezing him with her pelvic muscles making him come as well almost at the same time. He held her there for ages with what felt like gallons of hot come spurting into her making her squirm and wriggle with pleasure, then he carried her over to the bed and continued to take the rest of his clothes off and lay down beside her.

"Sorry" he said "I got a bit carried away then; it happens sometimes I just can't help it. Frustration with my life seems to build up in me and I just need an outlet, that's why I spend so much time at the gym trying to control my feelings and stop things like that happening. I'm not always that much of an animal in bed you know."

"I don't remember complaining" she replied "I like a man who knows what he wants and you certainly wanted it!"

"There's no denying that Pandora I just find you so unbelievably sexier but I have to admit I do need sex all the time, I am in a constant state of arousal and no longer wear underwear because I want to be ready whenever the opportunity arises so to speak" he admitted sheepishly

Pandora straddled him and lent over so that he had a birds eye view of her magnificent tit's in her low cut top as she had not as yet taken her clothes off :

"Rory" she said "Please don't be embarrassed by that, you sound just like my kind of man, always willing and what's more to the point always able so stop talking and put that back where it's meant to be" she demanded referring to the erection that was now nestling against her right thigh waiting to spring into action. They were both enjoying themselves more than they had for a long time they were both completely uninhibited creatures who needed passion to thrive and they had met their match in each other but what Rory didn't realise was for Pandora this was work, she was still busy filing away all the pillow talk and snippets of information she could gather for later reference, she had not lost sight of her main aim which was to make money and reek revenge on all men but she didn't mind having fun on the way at the expense of an already cheated and betrayed wife.

Rory lent forward and took her already hard little erect nipple into his mouth expertly flicking back and forwards and causing little darts of pleasure to course through her, she squirmed and felt her juices rush again, she was arching her back trying to reach down to grab hold of his balls and when she did she gave the hard little bullets they had become a sharp hard squeeze causing him to gasp and push up harder into her as he wriggled and squirmed trying to get away from her cruel gripping hand and hold onto his load at the same time, finally she gently tickled the soft dark skin under his scrotum and he couldn't take anymore he had to admit defeat as his body shuddered and relaxed and he lay back smiling telling her she was a whore in the bedroom. The best accolade that Pandora could have heard, always her aim to please where sex was concerned she felt proud and unnaturally pleased with herself. They continued like this for hours, stopping and starting taking each other to new heights and enjoying every minute of it but finally they had to admit defeat, they both needed sustenance and sleep in that order. They called for room services before they lay back and slept the deep sleep of the satisfied and replete.

Rory had made no secret of his marriage, he did not feel the need to hide it from Pandora as it was obvious to both of them that he was viewing her as a bit on the side, which was fine by her they both knew that neither of them was looking for stability or commitment and neither of them was expecting fidelity, they had realised they were too alike and had similar needs as soon as they had met. Rory liked fun and he saw in Pandora a woman who would indulge his every fantasy in the bedroom, look good on his arm and leave him alone when he needed peace and solitude or another woman to make life interesting, so he was quite happy for the affair to go on as long as he was enjoying himself. But he had underestimated Pandora, he had no idea she had a hidden agenda and she was happy for him to be kept unaware of her motivation and plans for the future. She had so far managed to keep stalling Janelle, telling her she had so far found no evidence of Rory's two timing and that she was still working on the case but Pandora had a shock coming, if Rory was underestimating Pandora then Pandora was sure as hell underestimating Janelle and she was soon to realise that mistake.

Janelle wasn't quite as nice as Pandora thought and she knew her own husband very, very well she was positive he was over the side and knew just the sort of people that were capable of pulling him back into line and making him aware that he had been caught out and punished, she had decided not to keep waiting for Pandora's report, she couldn't make her mind up if the girl was just incompetent or hiding something so she called her old employee and friend Paulie Santini for some help and advice.

Paulie Santini had officially been Janelle's financial advisor for many years but in truth he was a vicious henchman who kept his eye on her finances because he had originally been one of her financial backers back in the early seventies when she owned several London clubs and drinking dens and had helped her out in business and "personal issues" as he called them whenever required ever since. Personal issues to Paulie Santini meant whenever anyone needed a little poke or often a bloody great sledgehammer, and as the clubs were also running over three hundred girls in the prostitution trade Paulie's own special services had been required on a regular basis. Paulie had known Janelle from the early days when she had been put on the streets by her mother at twelve years old, she had clawed herself up from a life of degradation and abuse and she knew all the tricks of the trade in the profession she had chosen. She was not a Madam with a heart of gold she was cold evil and calculating and in those days she not only had the looks but she also had the knowledge of some of her girls more famous and powerful clients to go far and amass a personal fortune and database of people in both the business and criminal world who owed her dearly. Her girls were always in demand, they could cater for any kink or perversion in a customer's personality and any girl that didn't conform to Janelle's policy of "no holds barred" would find themselves out of a job if they were lucky. If they weren't they could find themselves either maimed or dead, if the client didn't manage it then Janelle knew people who would, as a last resort she was not adverse to getting her own hands dirty but felt that a woman in her position shouldn't have to so she surrounded herself with people who would do her dirty work for her, Paulie being her main man.

Amazingly almost everyone that knew Janelle Anstruthers now, knew nothing of her past, it wasn't that she had left that life behind years ago because she secretly still ran a ring of girls which not even Rory knew about but she figured with a husband like him she would always need a source of income however rich she was she also had a feeling of power running these girls and taking some of their hard earned money, she harboured a great regret that she was now too old to be getting some of the sex they were getting, paid or not. She had always found it exciting going from one man to another, taking what they needed to give and moving on to the next and she often had a little fantasy that her own husband was paying her girls for sex and not even realising it, she knew he was not beyond sleeping with prostitutes when the urge took him and she felt a little triumph that some of that money might be going into her own bank account. Rory was blissfully unaware of her criminal and violent past, she had changed physically, had all the scars surgically removed, everything lifted and tucked, changed her name and moved out to the suburbs since the days when she was a well known face and Rory would have been too young to remember anyway even if they had met in her previous life. She had attained everything she had wanted to by becoming someone else but her wayward husband was about to find out that although she was no longer Linda Gerrety, a name he had never heard from her lips, Linda Gerrety had not gone away, she just lurked underneath the surface and his lack of knowledge and fidelity would be his main regret for the rest of his life.

Chapter 6

Rory played hard, Pandora wasn't his only regular bit on the side, he also had an eighteen year old blonde holed up in a flat he paid for in Peckham south east London who he visited at least twice a week. Of course the money he paid with was indirectly from Janelle but Rory didn't have a conscious to worry with and the little blonde provided a warm bed and a lithe, young nimble body for him to play with to his heart's content. What Rory didn't know was that Janelle was quiet aware of this little girl and in her heart she was the one she was hoping Pandora would catch him with because although she had a heart of stone Rory was her one weakness and she tried to convince herself that if this girl was in fact the only one perhaps she could deal with the little tart without having to hurt Rory but at the back of her mind she knew that was impossible. At the end of the day too many people knew that Rory had been making a monkey of her and she knew in her heart of hearts she definitely could not stand for that.

Paulie was always there for her, at one point they had been lovers but that was when she was no more than a child and since her marriage to Rory although she often lamented the old days she had been 100% faithful, so now they were nothing but friends, the very best of friends he was one of the few people who knew her from the old days and was privileged enough to know her true identity, she trusted him with her life. They had always had one thing in common and that was their lack of moral code, and she needed him now. Many other men might bulk at what she was expecting him to do, but paulie was not one of those men, it broke her heart but Rory was a problem she no longer could ignore, she needed him sorted and she wanted it done now so Paulie was her man.

Paulie waited for him to leave Janie's little love nest late one night and followed him to his car in the underground car park where he had taken to leaving it out of sight on his many extra marital expeditions to her flat. Rory had never met Paulie and was unaware of his connection to his wife, he vaguely noticed the tall muscular man as he passed mainly because of the scare on his cheek, it looked angry and raised as if it had only happened recently and something in the mans eyes as their eyes locked made a shiver run up Rory's spine. Not usually one to be jumpy or intimidated he felt uneasy being anywhere near this man as if he had a premonition of his own fate. He dropped like a stone when the first bow hit him, it flicked through his mind that he must have been carrying a hammer of some sort but in truth it was Paulie's fist that had inflicted the crucial blow. Rory rolled onto his side and tried to protect his body with his arms, the smell of urine and oil mixing in his nostrils as he lay on the car park floor. The kicks to his head and upper body made the sickness roll up from his stomach and burn in his throat, his vision began to blur as blood flooded his eyes, he realised the high pitched keening he thought he could hear in the distance was actually coming from him and even in the midst of all the pain he saw this as weakness and tried to suppress the howling and deprive his attacker of the pleasure he must be getting from what he thought was an unprovoked attack. Rory's mind was in overdrive trying to think why this was happening to him and in his more lucid moments he came to the conclusion that it must have been all Janey''s fault. She was to blame, she must have been seeing someone else who had taken a dislike to sharing her lithe little body with him and that must be why this was happening, who else would want to hurt him?

Paulie was relentless in his attack, the red mist had descended and all he could think about was breaking this man's body and mind. He hated Rory with a passion for what he had done to his Janelle, Janelle that he adored and had seen the pain and suffering on her beloved face when she had asked for his help. He showed no mercy and wanted every bone in this man's body broken, left to him he would have made sure the scum was distinguished for good, but that wasn't what Janelle wanted, she wanted him alive so he would have to spare him for her sake or be the cause of more pain and suffering to the woman he would help with his dying breath.

Rory came round, realising he couldn't move his arms or legs he panicked and tried to shout for help but his voice would not come to him, his neck and head were so battered and bruised all he could manage was a whispered croak that even if there had been anyone around probably would have not managed to attract their attention. The car park was deserted, he lay on the floor covered in mud and blood his mind groping for instructions, willing it to tell him what to do next, he'd kill that bloody Janey for this, little whore why couldn't they ever learn to keep their knickers on and be grateful for what they were given? Why had she put him in this situation? Almost every bone in his body was broken but he immediately thought of his dick. What if she had given him something nasty? They never used condoms so what if she wasn't careful with other men's cocks what if he had a death sentence hanging over his head because of that stupid little fucker? At no time did it occur to him that he had been fucking around, that he never used condoms or that he had more to worry about than a sexual infection. He made his mind up to visit his private doctor as soon as he could, he had suffered because of his promiscuity before and he didn't intend to suffer that pain or humiliation again because of some loose legged little bimbo who didn't know when she was getting the best. All these thoughts were passing through his mind whilst he lay there praying for help to come, he didn't know how long he had been left laying there but when he woke up he was in a hospital bed, the constant bleep of the monitor and the dripping of the I.V breaking through the haze of the Diamorphine he had been pumped full of.. Janelle stood by the side of his bed with an almost serene look on her face, the way she looked after he had satisfied her in bed and she felt in power and control. The medics obviously took this as a look of pure relief that her husband had at last gained consciousness after 2 weeks in the land of the living dead but in that split second Rory knew the truth. He had finally realised that he had pushed his wife too far and that she had extracted a type of revenge he would never have felt her capable of, but he had more to learn about his wife than he had ever realised and she had in no way finished with him yet, not by a long chalk.

Chapter 7

Pandora had had a lucky escape, by the time she realised Rory was not coming back for more she had already decided to make her report to Janelle, to tell her she was right, her husband was indeed a horny bastard who was up for sex wherever and with whomever he could get it. Janelle had no idea that Pandora had been one of his conquests and had thought she had already dealt with the little whore he was screwing in Peckham. By the time she had finished with her no man would take a second look, female circumcision would have been kinder. Janey was because of her association with Rory doomed to a life of never feeling sexual pleasure again even if she did manage to get a man. It had given Janelle a real thrill when she read in the paper the report of the girl being dumped at the A and E Department of the Whittington, she had no fear of being traced as the perpetrator of the crime because she no longer had an identity, she lost that many years ago when she became Janelle, Janelle Anstruthers respectable business woman, Linda Gerraty was dead, she died in a fire along with her crimes, 10 years ago, Janelle Ansthruthers was a different person or she thought she was until now. The Queen was dead, long live the Queen.

Pandora filed her report, made up the bits she didn't know and walked away with her life unharmed, unaware what a lucky woman she was. Janelle paid her well and was blissfully in ignorance that Pandora had been screwing her husband for weeks whilst doing the job. Pandora was yet to find out that the man she had been sleeping with was laying barely alive in a hospital bed, he would never walk again, would never be able to give a woman the pleasure she had with him but worst of all he would never be able to leave his wife, he was now her prisoner which was what she had wanted in the beginning, for him never to be able to leave her as she aged and he was still young and virile.

Pandora was now on the look out for a new client and it didn't take long. There seemed to be a long list of suspicious wives who wanted evidence of their husbands infidelities or financial dealings and Pandora was loving it, she was getting all the uncomplicated sex she could handle, making a decent living and best of all crucifying her lovers by telling their wives they were over the side with some other woman. Leaving out the fact that she was the other woman, along with several others of course because men like that never only had one woman at a time which made it convenient for Pandora to leave her own part in the proceedings out of her reports. Weeks turned into months and as usual Pandora began to get bored with the life she had, she loved the excitement and the sex, she even loved the deceit but she felt she wanted more and yet again started to think about other things when a client with a difference turned up. This was one Pandora couldn't handle she needed someone who in her words was plain, mousy and unassuming. This one was into woman who had no confidence in themselves, he wasn't attracted to woman who spent hours in front of the mirror he wanted intelligence and sympathy so who did Pandora think of but me. I was the only person who she knew would fit the bill but she also knew I was the only one of her friends who would be unwilling to do it. Pandora set out to wear me down and get me to agree to make contact with the man who was named Toby, she explained that he was kind and gentle that their was no deep seated problems or violence involved, just the fact that his fiancé was paranoid and disillusioned with the relationship.

Pandora was like a dog with a bone, determined to get me to help her out, I felt pressured and at the same time a bit curious as to what it would feel like acting detective for a night. After weeks of her nagging I finally agreed to Pandora's demands on the grounds that this would be her last job, that the agency would fold and she would no longer put herself in danger of revenge attacks from either clients or ex-lovers and that she would never ever breath a word of my involvement to Wayne as long as she lived. For some reason she seemed to find this hilarious, she could not see that if he ever found out it would destroy my marriage because she had never had the type of relationship we did but she swore on her life she would never tell another living soul of my involvement, she reasoned it was only one drink, she would be around to observe and it didn't have to go any further, the fiancé was not accusing him of sleeping with other women, just trawling bars and clubs to talk to them. I was not happy but I thought it would work if that's all I had to do.

The night of the date I had never felt so guilty in my life. I had kissed Wayne goodbye as he went off on a night shift and started to get myself ready. It didn't take much preparation as Pandora had said no make up, just normal everyday clothes, nothing special just be myself, but I did need to have a couple of drinks to settle my nerves. Pandora turned up at six thirty with a bottle of red and set about calming me down. She knew me well enough to know I would be a nervous wreck and having second thoughts so she had come prepared with the wine and her best soothing nature. We talked for over an hour and polished off the wine and then we set off for the Red Lion in town. When we got inside Pandora headed for the bar and I took a seat by the window, I had not wanted to see the picture that Pandora had with her of Toby until we got here in case I got colder feet than I already had but when she pulled it out of her handbag I was surprised to see how handsome he was. For some reason I had expected him to be hideous, some sort of misfit who would find it hard to talk to women as Pan had said I would probably have to make the initial contact but he was really impressive. Short dark hair topped a face full of kindness, eyes that sparkled with mischief and a dazzling smile, I felt confused but Pandora just laughed and said she knew if I had seen the picture before we had arrived I would have run a mile. I looked around and realised Toby was already at the bar chatting away to another man about the same age, around thirty, deep in conversation about football, taking very little notice of his surroundings and concentrating on his companions words. I needed to get this over and done with as quickly as possible before I lost my nerve so I set off to the toilets which would take me into his path and used one of the oldest tricks in the book tripping up as I passed him and grabbing his arm for support.

After the contact had been made it was surprisingly easy to continue talking. We had a lot in common as to our backgrounds. Neither of us talked about our present home lives, I think we both realised the other shouldn't be doing what we were but so far it had only been talking. When I did finally make that trip to the toilet Pandora disentangled herself from the would be suitor who had attached himself to her and followed me in. she asked me if I would mind if she went, she had loads of other things to do and she said I was obviously at home with Toby and well able to look after myself and because I felt safe with Toby I said no, looking back I wished I hadn't but at the time I was carried away with the wine and company and was not thinking straight, Pandora left and I spent the rest of the night drinking and talking and getting to know Toby better. The night ended in what felt like the most natural thing in the world, going back to Toby's flat and spending the night together, the horror of what I had done to Wayne only hit me in the morning when the drink and excitement had worn off but amazingly there was still a spark between us. We both knew we would have to see each other again even though we knew we could end up hurting other people but we had started something we knew had a long way to run yet, or so I thought, I didn't bank on Pandora's spite and jealousy, I should have known better than trust her but unbeknown to me she had decided Toby had something she wanted a bit of. Ultimately this greed of her's would save my life but at this point it just felt like a huge betrayal and just another of Pandora's lusts for something someone else had.

Chapter 8

Jez had never forgotten the pain and humiliation he had suffered at Janelle's hands. His time working for her had been spent in fear and degradation, as he was only nineteen he never had the money or skills to escape her clutches and continued to suffer until he had gained the courage to get away and make a new life for himself. His mother had worked for Janelle when he was small, a drug addicted prostitute who used him as a punch bag through out his childhood and made his life a living hell. In and out of foster homes year after year at least he had a warm bed, food in his belly and the love most of these well meaning do gooders would provide, he never wanted to go home but he had a temper he could not control and sooner or later it would rear it's ugly head and his temporary carers would decide they couldn't cope with his behaviour any longer and back he'd be sent to Shirley, scared he would infect their own children with the poison gained from his mother and her friends, used as an example of how they could turn out if they followed in his footsteps and pushed from home to home and then back to the mother who despised him.

Jez was a constant reminder to her as to what put her on the game in the first place. A Dad that didn't want him and didn't even wait around long enough to see him come into the world and a Mum who blamed him for the break up of the relationship with the love of her life wasn't a good start in life. Shirley had become depressed and unable to cope after his birth and had turned to the drink and the drugs to get her through the day, blotting her problems out and sending her into oblivion where she could believe all was well in her little world and dream her dreams in peace and quiet. The habit she acquired had quickly spiralled out of hand and her social security money didn't cover her debts to her dealers. She had nothing else in the flat to sell, she had already sold everything that wasn't bolted down, no TV or stereo, no phone or even toys adorned the flat any longer, she was completely destitute all she had was her body which she would sell to anyone and everyone who had the money to pay for it, none of that money made it home but at least she could buy enough smack to make her happy.

Food wasn't a priority for Shirley, from an early age she would send Jez out begging outside the shops and the Tube station, if that failed he would be sent to steal food for himself and vodka for her, she didn't need much food and could never understand why he was always hungry, she always knew where her next hit was coming from but food for her Son just never seemed to cross her mind. If all else failed she could always give the old Asian bloke in the corner shop a freebie, she wasn't fussy, neither were her clients otherwise they wouldn't have touched her with a barge pole but whilst men still had dicks, she'd survive. She'd learnt long ago to shut off and just get on with it, close her mind to the sweat, smoke, old sex and urine, most of the men couldn't even piss straight, let alone know how to use their dicks properly, all they were interested in was a blow job or a quick shag against the wall down a dark alley after spending the day in the pub and before going home to a wife that wouldn't go near them let alone fuck them. She had learnt to finish them off quickly, that way she could do as many as ten a day if she needed more drugs and she always needed more drugs.

Shirley never felt it necessary to keep her working life away from her young Son. From three or four he would wake up in his filthy little room and know there was a strange man in the flat, he had developed a highly sensitive sense of smell and knew the subtle differences of human sweat and the rank smell of stale sex that hung over the flat all the time. That smell would never leave his nostrils for as long as he lived, that smell that made him obsessively clean, showering four or five times a day and not wanting or needing to have a sexual relationship since he was very young and unable to suppress his natural urges. He had seen the pain and suffering sex caused, spent his young life suffering its consequences and he had realised it had an element of weakness about it, and weakness in any form he could not stand. The pathetic creatures that used his mother were enslaved to their cocks, even the relatively normal ones who did need to use Shirley because of their sexual kinks and lust for deprivation had let sex ruin their lives, most had gone through divorces because their wives could not tolerate their visits to prostitutes, especially ones like his mother. He had been witness to some of their wrath himself a couple of times when they had found out where Shirley lived and come round to punch seven shades of shit out of her. She'd be battered and bruised, black eyes, missing teeth, broken Ribs; she was no match for most of these women. After they'd left she would just take another hit, slap more make-up on and be back on the streets by dark, never learning her lessons and taking anything any colour, creed or religion, any age or any condition, she'd take it all and it was never nice

Jez knew the local clap clinic well; after all he'd been visiting it with his mother since before he was born. She was a regular, all the staff knew her and she was often given VIP treatment, not needing to take a ticket and wait like the rest of the Toms and drug addicts that frequented its sickly yellow walls and toilets full of discarded needles, crack pipes and condoms. Shirley was famous for even fucking the doctor who took great pleasure in examining the women who came to him for help, he liked the fact that she would do literally anything for money but he never had to pay, she was so grateful for his help it was there for the taking. The sick bastard had even done it in front of Jez when he was about ten, not that it was new to him, he'd seen his Mother service her clients enough times to know what was what, once even being enlisted to hold the camera for one particularly twisted tourist who wanted a souvenir of his trip to London. Jez certainly hoped he had got that from his Mother, a good attack of Herpes would be a fitting present to take home for his wife or a dose of Crabs would have him scratching his balls for months and answer Jez's prayers.

Understandably Jez's relationship with his Mother was strained. Mostly she had no time for him, but when she had run out of drugs and was feeling low she would want him to play the dutiful Son. She would want his love and attention, cuddle him, tell him how sorry she was and that deep down she loved him with all her heart. She would try to convince him she was doing it all for him, but Jez knew differently, he knew that all that was self pitying bullshit, that she cared about no one but herself and that since he had been born she had hardly given him a second thought. She was one of those women who always felt sorry for themselves, she could not see that most of her problems were of her own making and was always looking for someone else to blame and as the years went on that person was more and more Janelle Anstruthers, or Linda Gerraty as she knew

Auntie Linda was always a welcome visitor, taking time to sit and talk to him, bringing gifts of toys and food and generally brightening his very dull life. He didn't realise at first that she also brightened his Mothers life but for other reasons, it was much later on that he realised why his Mother was so happy when Linda had visited and that was why he not only mistrusted her as he got older but began to hate her. 'Auntie Linda' had been supplying Shirley with some of her more unsavoury specialist clients for years and along with her visits came payment from these freaks of nature and huge amounts of Heroin and Cocaine. At that time in her life

Shirley had been coherent enough to be of some use to Linda, she distributed the goodies that Linda supplied to some of the other girls on the estate, Shirley still had her looks and Linda liked her to double up with some of the less experienced girls, show them the ropes and introduce them to the drugs that would help them deal with their clients demands and line Linda's pockets with the profit, Shirley was too stupid to realise that she should be feathering her own nest and the sweat and blood her lifestyle caused her should be invested for her own future not an evil bastard like Linda's.

When Linda stopped visiting was when things went from bad to worse, Shirley had no regular supplier for either the men or the drugs so she had no choice but to start working the street, street corners and back alley's became her only source of income and the hatred both she and Jez felt for Linda became their only common emotion. Jez had always been able to see that Linda was using Shirley but she had also made her happy but Shirley had not realised that as soon as another tart came along that could be of use to Linda Shirley would be out on her ear. Younger, prettier and more compliant, less drug ravaged and eager Shirley was redundant and hated Linda for her betrayal. Jez was not as stupid as his Mother he had seen it coming but he hated her for the fact that a life that was already a misery had become a complete nightmare.

Chapter 9

His Mother was dependant on him for almost everything in those early days. When she had run out of drugs and could not work she was worse than a baby. He was ten years old and he had to get her up in the morning, invariably having to change the bed where she had pissed or vomited in the night and didn't have the energy or the will to make it to the bathroom or even the bucket he would leave by the bed. He would wash her, dress her and try to get her to take some food, feeding her like an invalid, begging her to eat as even with his young eyes he could see she was wasting away in front of him. He hated it, he detested every last minute of it, he couldn't remember the last time he went to School, even the truancy officer had stopped calling, frightened of his Mother's temper and lack of cooperation. The Social Services had enough and quietly retreated hoping the problem would disappear, that by some chance Shirley would kill herself or be murdered or Jez would run away to someone else's patch and become their problem. This little family had caused them too much trouble over the year's, they had lost patience and given up trying to help. They could recognise a disaster waiting to happen when they saw one and didn't want to be involved and end up taking the flack as incompetent slackers.

Jez wasn't a good thief, looking back he was never really sure if he wanted to get caught or if he just didn't have the knack. At least when he got caught he would get some of the attention he craved. At the police station someone else was in charge, someone else was in control and he was expected to act like the child that he was. They were nice to him at the station they would give him hot chocolate and biscuits or coke and crisps, he wasn't used to being given things, he was only used to having to get them himself one way or another. They would make a young P.C sit with him and keep him talking, wrap him in a grey scratchy blanket and often have a private little collection because they felt sorry for him which meant it was one of the rare occasions he had money in his pocket. They would pamper him and make him feel important until someone from Social Services came to collect him and take him to the children's home, he liked these homes, he had other children to play with and talk to. Not children that had normal loving parents but children like himself who had dysfunctional families, no one who really cared for them and they would form friendships and allegiances because they understood each others survival instincts. The homes were comfortable and had lots of games and toys to play with and for a little while he was a child again. No responsibilities, no worries and no dependant Mother to suck the life out of him and make him old before his time. But he could find no peace in the end she wouldn't let him.

As soon as Shirley was sober enough she would realise that he wasn't there looking after her, that the cupboards were empty, that she was sleeping in her own filth and that she needed his companionship, just another human being sharing the same space so that she knew she wasn't actually dead, that she had woken up in the morning and that she still had some tenuous link to the outside world, then she would go and bring him back. Shirley knew how to stay clean when she really needed to and that's what she'd do. No drugs for a couple of weeks, clean the house, get food in the cupboard and convince her Social worker she had made an effort. The Social worker didn't believe for a minute that she intended to stay clean but at the end of the day they couldn't be bothered to argue, he was her Son, they had other children waiting for his space in the home and she wanted him back, so they handed him back. Jez had no say in the matter but he wasn't sure he would refuse to go back anyway he had a heart and a conscience. He didn't know where he had got them from but there again the only family he knew was his Mother, no other relatives had ever come forward to claim him, he didn't even know if he had any other family, he knew he must have had a Dad at some point but he never knew what had happened to him, just that he had left, he didn't know his name or if he was still alive even. Jez only had his Mother and he felt responsible for her so he kept going back as soon as she asked and the nightmare would start again and at the back of it all, the root of all the problems in his young mind was Linda Gerraty.

Once Linda disappeared he felt like he'd been abandoned, for all her faults she had always shown a motherly streak to him and made him feel special. She would sit him down on the sofa and give him the presents she would bring she would talk to him in a soothing voice, ask him what he had been up to and take an interest in his life, it didn't feel like she was being nosey like when the Social worker or police asked it felt like she was a friend truly interested in his wellbeing. Linda would never let him see the money or drugs she was giving his mother, it was Shirley that always told him that she treated him like a child who should be protected and shielded from the harsher side of life but that was the contradiction in her personality, on the one hand she was helping to make his life what it was but on the other she was trying to compensate for it at the same time. It was many years before he found out why she behaved in this way with him, that she had a Son of her own about the same age and that for his own sake she had given him up many years before when her own life had been worse than his own Mothers was now. For the next few years nothing changed much for Jez or his Mother. His behaviour became worse, he was running around the streets committing burglaries, muggings anything that would put money in his pocket and food on the table and his Mother continued to ply her trade. His own life had been blighted by her choice of career and he had to learn to look after himself and stand up for his own reputation. At times he had also had to avenge his Mothers clients who refused to pay her for services rendered or who inflicted injuries and pain too much for him to watch her bear but in the main part he only did what he had to. He did not enjoy the criminal life and was saving hard to get away from it but in the meantime his Mother still had to be looked after and there was no way he could afford her drug habit so she had to continue to work even though she couldn't manage to get the amount of clients she used to. Any looks she once had been lost to the drugs and prostitution so she continued to service the dregs of society and be defiled by every misfit within twenty miles. But things were about to change. Linda Gerraty was about to come back into their lives and that would do no one any good.

Linda walked back into their lives as if she had never left, as large as life, twice as successful and throwing money around like there was no tomorrow. In the last five years she had gone from strength to strength leaving the common tart trade and opening nightclubs in London and the north of England. She had become reacquainted with an old flame called Paulie Santini and between them they were making money hand over fist, they still ran girls in the clubs under the names of escorts and as with all the clubs in the eighties drug use was rife. Paulie and Linda turned a blind eye but took a cut from the dealers and the local vice and drugs squads were given preferential treatment drinks and girls wise so they were happy and kept out of the way. Life was good, money in the bank, no worries and Linda had loved Paulie from the first time she had met him. Linda had come back for a reason though and that reason was Jez. She had always had a soft spot for the boy and when she started to hear he was making a name for himself she decided she would like to go back and see how he was doing, see if he could be of use to her and in her own way give him a hand to get on in life. It didn't seem to bother her that the only way she could help him was by getting him further entrenched in crime, she had long been able to forget that that was what her business was; she had sanitised it in her own mind. Linda had come to believe that because she no longer laid with dogs she had never had fleas which of course was a total lie, Linda had been one of the hardest perverted prostitutes in London, many a man had crossed her and come to regret it and many a woman including Shirley still bore the scares from some of Linda's own ex-clients when she had decided her own body could take no more and now she had turned her eye to Jez she had just the right job for him and she set out to lure him into her web with the money and power she now possessed.

Chapter 10

Pandora saw Jez as a challenge, she had never met a man that could not resist her before and it aggrieved her that he had no interest in her whatsoever. She had tried for months to get him to make a move on her but he seemed not to care about women at all which led her to believe he was bent. Mind you she came to this conclusion about any man who took longer than 48 hours to get into her knickers, so she set about trying to change his sexual preferences as she saw them, but with Jez this was never going to work. His Mother had left him so emotionally scared that the only two proper relationships he had with women had ended in disaster and as soon as he was disciplined enough to not need sex any longer he was happier in himself. He liked working for Pandora, he liked sorting out the girls problems, after all he'd been sorting out his Mothers problems all his life and he was good at it. Most of them were nice girls, conceited airheads but what could you expect from models, self obsession was their reason for living. The scrapes they got themselves into were mainly either financial or choosing the wrong boyfriends who wouldn't take no for an answer when the girls had enough of them, nothing too complicated. A quick visit, a few slaps in the right place and they usually got the message, nothing along the lines he used to have to do for Linda Gerraty when he worked for her.

Life was sweet now, so why was he still so unhappy in his own skin, why did he still have this burning desire to find Linda Gerraty again and extract revenge for everything that had happened in both his and his Mother's lives. Why did he feel there was unfinished business that he would never fully settle until he knew it had all come to an end, after all Linda was dead wasn't she? She had died in a fire a long time ago hadn't she? The problem was he never believed that she had died, he personally had not identified the body and the only way he could have believed she was truly dead was if he had been given that privilege, if he had been allowed to see the bitch on a mortuary slab, cold lifeless and no longer a threat to anyone. He didn't believe such evilness could be extinguished so easily, he knew in his bones that she was still alive, still walking this Earth whilst his Mother had been laying in a Hospital bed for near on ten years. Shirley was now unrecognisable as the woman she had once been, tubes coming out of every orifice, narcotic drugs being pumped into her from numerous drips, which was ironic really as she never could get enough smack, she had spent her whole life being ruled by drugs, working the streets, stealing hurting just to slake her constant craving and now she was getting them free on the NHS. She now had a constant drip, drip, drip of amphetamines, morphine and heroin substitute shooting round her veins, no withdrawal, no cravings just constant oblivion which was what she had always aspired to, what she had ruined both her own and his life for and now she had it in spades. In his darker moments he had wished she had crossed Linda earlier, perhaps his own life would have been easier, he would have stayed in one of the homes or with one of the foster families, maybe someone would have even adopted him and he could have had a better life, a normal life, he might even have been normal now if that had happened. He may not be living a sterile isolated life now with no hope of ever having a normal sex life or emotional support if she had made her mistake earlier and he might have had a chance instead of only being capable of one emotion, and that was pure unadulterated hate and only for one person. Linda Gerraty.

Jez still visited his Mother, he didn't really know why, she didn't know him, she was a shrunken mass of suppurating sores, kept clean and warm but her body was eating her away from the inside out. The face he had known as a child just a fused scarred mass of bubbled flesh where the acid had hit and boiled the skin almost clean off the bones, her nose almost unrecognisable it had been broken so many times and in so many places, no hair, hair follicles couldn't grow to the parched paper thin skin that was left on her skull and her teeth had long ago fallen out from neglect or constant blows. He had swallowed his pride and begged them to let her go, to stop the suffering and let her slip away but the Doctor said this wasn't possible, that until her organs failed and her body showed signs of giving up they had an obligation to feed her life sustaining fluids and drugs to keep her out of pain, to keep her hanging on to her thread of a life, just in case there was a dramatic change in her condition, in case her brain decided to come out of it's suspended state and start controlling her body again. He had sat by her bed for many hours just wishing he could find the courage to disconnect the tubes himself, turn the life support machine off or place a pillow over her face but he just could not do it, he couldn't just kill the only person that had ever belonged to him, even though she had made him what he was, he wished he could harness that pure hatred he felt for Linda and use it to help his mother leave this world but he couldn't do it. He wanted her to go but he could never be the one to do it, so he visited her a couple of times a month, sat by her bed, talked to her, asked the Doctor's if there was any change knowing the answer would always be the same. He would leave with a heavy heart and the feeling that he was a complete failure, after all he had helped enough people off this mortal coil before their time but he could not help his Mother, he couldn't do it now and he knew he never would.

Shirley's betrayal of Linda in the end had been unintentional. For years she had always creamed a bit off the top, short changed whoever she was acting as go between for, pocketing a tip or swearing that a punter had short changed her, but Linda knew that, let Shirley think that she was being clever, allowed her a little victory here and there but some of the other girls weren't as lenient with her. If they were wired enough and needed every last grain of their hit they would take it out on Shirley whether it were her fault or not. Even then Shirley's body was a wreck, most of the girls she did business with knew they could anilhate her if they so wished. Many of them were new to the drugs and the game, were still fit and relatively healthy, many had the advantage of age and a upbringing of good food which made them strong and fast. A lot of the new girls had either become embroiled with drugs or prostitution through stupidity not necessity and many of them took Shirley to task with their fists over her gluttony for the drugs but Linda let her be. Linda didn't see a point to confronting Shirley, she could afford the relatively small amounts she took, she no longer used herself, she'd been clean for years and although she paid Shirley well for her services she knew everyone needed a perk, something they feel they deserve on top of what their given, something they feel they've earned in their own right but in the end she couldn't turn a blind eye to Shirley's misdemeanours, she couldn't lose face and respect from the rest of her troops so revenge had to be taken but Linda was never straight forward, revenge wouldn't be swift, it would be slow in coming but when it did the consequences would rock all their worlds.

Chapter 11

Jez had witnessed many of the attacks on Shirley when he was young but as he grew older he wouldn't stand by and watch it happen, he refused to have any part in Shirley's dodgy dealing and never touched drink or drugs but he would knock anyone into the middle of next week who touched Shirley once he was old enough to realise what was going on. No one who knew them could understand his fierce loyalty to his Mother after the life she had given him but at the same time they had to respect it. Not only was he a force to be reckoned with as he kept him self super fit and was as sharp as a knife and as quick as a greyhound he also had a temper that he couldn't control, once you had unleashed that temper it didn't matter how hard you thought you were you would end up regretting it. The mist descended and the only person who wasn't frightened of him was his Mother. Shirley took great pride in letting people know that she was the only one who could control her Son when he was in this condition but in truth that was not so. Jez controlled himself where Shirley was concerned, he certainly had nothing to respect her for and definitely had no reason to want to please her or fear her, and he just found her pathetic. He could no more hit her than a new born baby, he had a strict moral code which he supposed he must of inherited from his unknown Father and he only ever hurt people that had hurt him or his own when he was young, things would change when he became one of Linda's henchmen but at this time in his life he was the original honest villain living by the motto an eye for an eye a tooth for a tooth. When he had exploded with temper and inflicted pain and suffering on people he would skulk away on his own like a wounded animal ashamed of his actions and swearing never to allow himself to become so feral again, although not a believer in God he would prey that he could change and ask forgiveness making sure no one on this earth saw his remorse and desperation. But that was all before Linda.

Linda liked young men, after years of having to put up with the low life's and perverts who paid for her services she liked firm young bodies. She liked lads who looked after themselves, went to the gym, toned their muscles and smelt nice. She liked them to be vain and cocksure of themselves, to have young girls falling at their feet, to know that they were desired, to walk with a swagger and to know that they can have the pick of the women around them. The fact that they needed sex that their hormones were racing around their young bodies making them hard every time they looked at a woman also turned her on. Linda loved the fact that they needed to shag and that she could shag them whenever she wanted and however she wanted. For most of her life she had been the giver, she had been paid to please and if she hadn't supplied what was required she would suffer the consequences either physically or financially but now she was in control and liked to surround herself with young men who were always willing and more to the point able to fuck whenever she wanted them to. Boys always wanted to please an older woman and she had enough to know. They wanted to learn and experiment with their older lovers and Linda liked to teach. She was helping to teach the sadist's and perverts of the future and some women would suffer all their lives for their lovers and husbands learning their skills at the hands of Linda Gerraty. Some women would never recover from the beatings, the rape and the degradation their men had learnt to inflict from Linda and she took an evil pleasure in the fact that she was making these boy's into what they would become as men and none of them were nice loving Husbands and Fathers, she took great pride in what she taught them and revelled in the fact that she was playing a huge part in making other women who had never lived the life she had been forced to, suffer a little of what she had to endure in her young life. She had it all now, she had Paulie Santini her old friend, lover and constant companion to provide her with the love and support she needed as well as the sex that came attached to love, but he understood that it wasn't always sex and love she wanted, sometimes it was pain, sex that had no emotion and raw lust. He understood that she had been used to this all her life and that in an odd way she had become addicted to the pain and guilt and she thrived on it. At this stage in their relationship he was not willing to treat her like this, so she had to look elsewhere and this was when the scales fell from her eyes. Jez's reputation on the estates had been growing over the last couple of years but she had still been seeing him as little more than a child. When it came to her attention one day that he had executed a particularly vicious attack on another boy who had crossed him she suddenly realised that the fresh meat she craved constantly was closer to home than she had realised and she decided there and then that Jez would come and work for her whether he liked it or not and that she would enjoy fucking him stupid into the bargain.

Jez was easy prey to Linda, although hard as nails she knew his weaknesses, she had after all known him since he was a baby, known his Father, seen the way he had suffered due to his Mother's lifestyle and for many years had been the one person in his life to show him love and affection. She had lost count of the amount of times she had held him as a child when his Mother was too out of it to care that he was hurting, the only one to remember his birthday, to buy him presents, make sure there was food in the cupboard when he was in his Mother's care and not being looked after by some social worker or foster family. Linda knew everything about him and all of a sudden she realised that he had become what she liked, young, fit, ruthless and she wanted him. She wanted to make him the next Paulie Santini, maybe even replace him in the future as he was getting past it now in her mind but for the moment most of all she wanted his body not his soul that would come later.

Jez would never forget the way it first began. He was sitting at home, thinking out his next move to increase the money he was stashing away for his future away from his Mother, the estate and all its memories and what it represented. He'd already hit the odd Off Licence, Taxi Driver and corner shop which at his young age was already an impressive portfolio to have under his belt but he needed more and he needed it quickly. He had recently heard of a local hard man drug dealer who had lost his right hand man, run over and killed by a disgruntled smack head and Jez was set on taking his place. He figured this could be a real coup. Not only was he sure he could cream enough off the top to keep his Mother supplied and stop her hawking her arse all over town he was sure he could make a good living out of the dealer who was known for his generosity to his employee's as long as they were good and Jez knew that although only sixteen he was very good, very good indeed. When he looked up Linda was in the room, she had always had the ability to enter a room without alerting the occupants to her presence, like a cat slinking into a room to pounce on your lap before you've had time to kick it out again. He didn't know why because he had always got on well with Linda but tonight he was uneasy. She was dressed differently, gone was the sharp business suite, the pristine cotton blouse and the stiletto heels, tonight she was casual in a way as if she were trying to look younger than her 40 years. The jeans were designer of course but a plain tight white T-shirt and linen jacket showed off her figure nicely, her hair was loose and had been cut in a flattering Bob framing her face and the flat pumps she was wearing made her look small and vulnerable. Jez had never seen Linda without make up before and he was quite shocked how pretty she was. In the past he had always thought she had a hard immobile face but tonight he felt a stirring in his groin which even though young wasn't an everyday experience. He had always taken sex when he needed it, he didn't have much experience because he didn't often feel the need to shag. He didn't often even feel the need to wank like most boy's his age, he was already learning to control that desire and beginning to see it as a weakness in those who couldn't.

"Linda I wasn't expecting you, Mum's on the bash as usual."

"I know that Jez, I wanted to see you tonight" he felt that involuntary jerk in his balls again and stood up.

"I'll put the kettle on, there's nothing else in the house she drank it all before she left!"

"No change there then!"

Jez went out into the kitchen and switched the kettle down, he wanted to rub his groin to try and ease the ache that was building but he daren't in case it excited him more, it was a new experience for him to feel so vulnerable and he didn't like it. Linda entered the kitchen behind him. She noticed how clean and well stocked the cupboards were now Jez had taken over the household, in the past you couldn't enter this room for the rank smell of sour milk, rotting food and dirt, but now you could have eaten your dinner off the floor.

"Jez I want you to work for me!"

"Doing what Linda"

"You know the business Jez mostly protection for the clubs, I know you don't like the drugs side of things so I'd keep you away from them unless I needed major enforcement"

"Door man?"

"No not door man, for one thing you're too young, I'd never get you a licence and you know the clubs are almost legit now, I want you to work with me. You've got more nouse than most of my apes put together and you know it, I need someone with brains as well as muscle."

"What money are you talking? I'm making a bomb now, why would I take a drop just to work for you Linda. I know you've been good to me but I'm not a charity."

"Fuck you Jez, I'm not asking you for any favours you of all people should know that's not my style, I don't do any and I don't ask for any."

"Calm down I'm just getting things straight from the start, give me a price and I'll give you an answer."

"You are one cocky little fucker Jeremy. Dragged up by a street dog of a Mother, a Father you've never even met and you're giving me this shit. You really do make me piss myself sometimes"

"And don't you love me for it Linda, it's what makes me what I am!"

"O.k., o.k. how about we talk money after I've tried you out, I've got a serious debtor coming in the club tonight, he needs a frightener how about I observe and see how much I think your worth?"

"How about you observe and double what you first think of, you already know what I can do, you have your eyes and ears on the estate and you know full well I have about as much conscience as you do so let's not fuck about."

"Let's just get going to the club and I'll make it worth your while you'll get more than I'm paying anyone else as long as you give me everything I need and your definitely be getting more from me than you would for that arsehole Gary Doherty. I know he wants you but I want you more and I intend to get you Jez so please let's leave and get tonight out of the way before we make big plans for the future."

Jez left the room and headed for the Bathroom. He had no intention of starting his new career without looking his best so Linda would just have to wait for his services. He just hoped that he could control his dick long enough to get this nights work done

Chapter 12

Jez was feeling good about himself as he washed and changed preparing himself for the nights work. Violence always gave him a huge adrenaline rush he thrived on it and found the anticipation thrilling. He had left the bathroom door open as he shaved so he could carry on talking to Linda, discussing the man he was to put the fear of God into and make sure he honoured his debts for the use of the girls and the drugs. He thought he could take liberties because he helped Linda out now and again from the cellar of his own pub when she ran dry but that wasn't how it worked. Linda felt he was stretching the friendship too far, she always paid for his favours and made sure he suffered no agg from the old bill or any likely faces on the manor out to make a name for themselves so she felt he could treat her with the respect she deserved and pay for what and who he used. Jez had the job of teaching him that respect and making sure he never crossed the line with Linda again. She didn't want him outed, just scared and respectful so she would fill in Jez on what she wanted. Jez sensed that his and Linda's friendship had changed tonight and he liked the easy going atmosphere that was developing between them. He now knew she wanted him, he'd have to have been stupid not to realise it but when most girls showed their interest he just couldn't reciprocate, couldn't be asked but Linda was making him feel horney tonight and she knew it. He walked back into the living room where she was sitting on the sofa drinking her coffee; she stood up and kissed him on the cheek.

"Thank you Jez, thank you for giving this a try"

Jez turned his head and kissed her back on the lips both felt the spark of excitement between them and they both knew that would not be the end of it tonight. The atmosphere was thick with sexual attraction and as they walked out of the flat together Linda gave his back just between his shoulder blades a light stroke sending shivers from the top of his head all the way down to his coccyx making him aware of just how sexy she made him feel.

Linda's car was waiting downstairs, one of her usual drivers sitting at the wheel. As soon as he saw Linda in his rear view mirror he jumped out to open the door for her but Jez stepped forward and moved him aside making it obvious that he felt proprietarily towards Linda which shocked the driver, Jez was only a kid and Linda was letting him behave as if he was the big man. Paulie wouldn't like that, he couldn't wait to get rid of his passengers and report the latest to the man that was giving him a huge wedge to keep an eye on his boss and report back to her main man. Paulie didn't mind her having other men in fact sometimes he found it hard to keep up with her so it gave him a rest or a chance sometimes to fuck something younger now and again, Linda was only happy when she was well and truly satisfied in bed but Jez was something different. Jez was an up and coming face, a true contender for top man so Paulie definitely would not be happy. But the driver was happy that he would be in for a nice fat bonus when he passed this little nugget of information on and he was already spending it in his minds eye.

Jez and Linda chatted amiably all the way to the club her hand resting lightly on his knee. So far it had been unsaid but Jez was well aware of what was expected of him after he had sorted the main business of the night and he was looking forward to it. For some reason he suddenly needed to fuck, to perform like a rutting stag and rid himself of all the pent up frustrations he was feeling over his responsibilities to his Mother and he knew that Linda would be more than capable of taking what he needed to give. She had spent too many years on the game not to know every trick in the book, she needed sex like a duck needed water and tonight so did he. Her thumb kept straying to his crutch almost imperceptibly rubbing, making him squirm and wriggle and she began to whisper in his ear what she would like to do with him. Oh yes he knew what he was in for tonight which fired him up even more and made him impatient to get his work over with. When they reached the club Linda slipped back into professional mode. She ordered Jez to go in the front entrance but quickly went around the back to change into her work wear and slap on her mask. She would never allow her customers to see her as she was now, she wouldn't let them see her vulnerable look that was reserved for when she was trawling for fresh blood and she'd already got her hooks in her prey for tonight. She was almost licking her lips with excitement thinking of how that fresh young cock would taste when she took it into her mouth and sucked it dry. How she'd squeeze his balls until he screamed with pleasure and pain, she might even use her arsenal of toys, she didn't needed them but some men liked them. She would decide that later, whether to give him all the sweets in the sweet shop at once or whether to save some for next time, they had plenty of time, she had decided that she had no intention of this being a one night stand, she wanted this to run and run until she'd bled him dry and taught him all she knew, she would be the one to decide when it finished but in the meantime she had better get out on the floor and act the genial host whilst she watched proceedings unfold.

Jez was at the bar when she got back outside sipping mineral water and making conversation with a few known faces. Although only a boy with a fresh young face people always assumed he was older because of his maturity and ability to hold his own. The face she wanted sorted hadn't arrived yet but she didn't want to be seen too close to Jez so she did the rounds and made sure everyone knew her whereabouts in case she needed an alibi later. The mark came in and as luck would have it, stood right next to Jez, he was not yet well enough known for the debtor to be wary and he struck up a conversation about some of the tom's plying their trade and what he would like to do with them. Jez went along with the pretence and told the punter he ran some girls of his own, he'd baited the hook and the punter told him he was looking for something strange, he'd used Linda's girls so often at her expense he'd worked his way through her current crew and was looking for something different. Jez felt nothing but contempt for the fool, not only did his dick rule his brain he was stupid enough to leave a dodgy club with someone he knew nothing about, but who knew he had money burning a hole in his pocket. Jez had to smile to himself as he led the idiot outside, he wasn't young, he'd been around the pub and club scene for years and yet he still didn't have a clue, where did wankers like him come from. Another planet or did they just think that because they mixed with the big boys they were invincible; this was going to be so easy he could cry.

Jez had the good sense to lead him away from the club, he had already noted a car he would be able to lift but even that wasn't necessary the prat was willing to use his own wheels, this bloke was unfucking believable. He got him to drive to Walthamstow, far away enough from the west end for it to be hard to place his whereabouts, told him to cut the engine not far from the dog track and said they needed to walk to the flat from there. He said the girl was respectable, didn't want the neighbours seeing strange cars pulling up and of course the sad bastard swallowed it hook, line and sinker. He had wanted someone who was new to the bash and hadn't been around the block more than a couple of times so the respectable story went down well and Jez was pleased with his quick thinking. The excitement was building for both of them as they passed the deserted entrance to the track, the punter was babbling on about his weird fantasies but Jez was hardly listening his own excitement was becoming unbearable the adrenaline pumping through his veins, the blood rushing to his head he was ready, he was well and truly ready and he was going to enjoy this. He pulled the lump of lead piping from down the side of his right trouser leg with a flourish, he had concealed it there earlier at the flat and even Linda hadn't realised he was carrying he'd put so much practice into moving the weapon around and concealing it all over his body, he knew the day would come when he would need it and he intended to be a master at using it. He smashed the bar down across the other man's shoulders with such force he fell to his knees without a fight. he was not out to kill, just to frighten so he had to contain his anger and make sure he didn't overstep the line. He didn't mind killing, he had no compunction about that but he didn't want to screw up his first job for Linda, he wanted it clean, efficient, to ensure the man knew he had been well punished but at the same time that Jez had shown him mercy and he had had a lucky escape. He changed tactic and after wiping the pipe clean, he threw it as far away as possible, his victim was in too much pain and fear to move so he took his time, aimed a few kicks at his ribs, broke his arm, snapped his ankle and all the time letting him know why he was receiving the treatment that he was a ponce a waster and that taking liberties wouldn't be tolerated by Linda's firm. He rolled him over and took what money he had as a down payment on his debts and left him crying in the dirt, sobbing like a baby pleading for mercy. What he didn't know was that Jez had also called an ambulance, directed them to this pathetic excuse for a man, thrown him a lifeline; it would be stored up in his favour for when this nonce recovered. In all honesty the bloke hadn't murdered anyone, he'd taken what he thought he deserved, thought perks came with the job and that he merited being looked after but he knew different now, he had no conscience but he wasn't evil either he couldn't leave the bloke for dead over a minor piss take. He called the ambulance, called a cab and went back to Linda, older, wiser and feeling on top of the world.

Chapter 13

Jez went back to the club. For some unknown reason by the time he had got there his earlier feeling of euphoria had disappeared. The man hadn't even bothered to put up a fight, he had just taken the punishment and whimpered and cried like a little boy, once the adrenaline had stopped rushing his blood stream at high speed he came down like a stone. He felt depressed he needed to see Linda but she was keeping her distance, still circulating still making sure there would be no comeback on her if all this went off, no blame, too many people had seen her around tonight for the finger to point in her direction and even if anyone could say she was involved, they wouldn't too many people had crossed Linda and lost, in her clubs you kept your head down and your mouth shut then you lived to see another day. Jez sat down with one of the girls he vaguely knew through his Mother, it was playing on his mind he had his faults but he wasn't a bully, he liked a fair fight and he felt like a bullying shit, he'd been on the end of that enough at school and realised that he had just behaved in the same way as his tormentors had when he was just a little boy in the playground with a Mother who was a drug addled prostitute and an absent Father, no one to protect him, no one to give a shit about where he was or what was happening to him. The girl was chattering on, he wasn't really interested but tried to make the right noises in the right places, for her part she knew he wasn't a punter and she had a bloody great gas bill waiting to be paid so wasn't exactly finding him thrilling company either, she needed a trick fast, she had three kids at home, the electricity had already been cut off last month so the poor little bastards couldn't even watch the telly while she was out hauling her arse, Jez was not going to be the answer to her prayers, he had the look of a man that didn't need to pay for sex. She liked him, he was young, good looking and usually a good laugh but tonight she needed a walking wallet, all Jez needed was someone to kill some time with until Linda gave him the nod. He was getting agitated he wasn't used to dangling on someone else's string he wanted to talk to her and move on get the nights business finished and go home.

Jez looked across at Linda again, this time she gave him an almost undetectable movement of her head gesturing that he should make his way upstairs to the office. He was surprised to find there was no security of any kind leading up the dark two flights but he supposed that the people that got this far knew not to take liberties. He entered the office and realised it was almost masculine in style with it's huge walnut desk and chesterfield sofa's, it's shelves of books and subdued lighting reminded him of the one time he had visited the library with the school. He had been surprised that he liked it there, it was quiet and calm something he wasn't used to at home, the people all looked happy and normal and he found books which interested him, books that fired his imagination and showed him how the other half lived. He located the drinks cabinet and poured himself a large scotch, something he never done was drink alcohol but he needed something, his nerves where jangling and he needed to calm down, he sat down on one of the large leather sofa's and switched on the huge TV hanging on the wall to his right. The boxing was still on, it wouldn't do much to calm him down but at least it took his mind off of earlier and focused his thoughts on something other than his own behaviour. He wished Linda would hurry up, he was surprisingly nervous but he didn't have to wait too long. When she entered she told him straight away that she knew how the night had gone well, that she was pleased with his work but unhappy that he had felt the need to call an ambulance. He held his ground and refused to be intimidated by her, he told her she had not given him specific instructions and had left it up to him made it clear that as she wanted her money back he felt it would be pointless to kill or disable the bloke otherwise she would end up out of pocket when he couldn't graft to get her money for her. She had to laugh at his balls and he heaved a sigh of relief, he'd got away with it. He knew she hadn't been happy when she found out about the call but he'd taken a chance, he had his own code of practice to perfect after all, it was a good night's work and he was counting his blessings along with his money.

The business over it was time for the pleasure to begin. Linda straddled him as she placed his reward in his shirt pocket. She hoisted up her skirt and made it evident she was wearing no knickers just stockings and suspenders. She ground her sex down onto his eager crotch and wriggled around until she could feel his hardness through his clothes. Jez wanted to play it cool but his dick had other ideas as he began to squirm and buck against her, not a word passed between them as her hand shot down and she began to deftly release his straining cock, he had her blouse off of her shoulders and was squeezing her tit's much harder than he normally would but she seemed to be enjoying the pain, he buried his face in her neck breathing in the sweet cloying smell of her poison perfume, he needed to be inside her now, he didn't know how much longer he could last and he didn't like the lack of control he felt. He thrust violently upwards and she gasped as all good actresses do and began to rock rhythmically backwards and forwards riding him as hard as she could, she squeezed her thighs together to cause more pressure and tensed her pelvic muscles so that he filled her up completely. Although he was not small Linda was well used and even though she had indulged herself with surgery to tighten things up and the surgeon was a miracle worker, his name wasn't Jesus and he couldn't make a silk purse out of a sow's arse, he had explained he could only do so much with the material he was given, a work man is only as good as his tools. Jez could hold back no more she knew that he had gone about as far as he could so she lent backwards and gave a sharp yank on his balls, he jerked involuntarily and shot his load deep inside her shuddering to a climax and collapsing with the exertion, his breathing ragged and cold sweat running down his back, he was stunned, shell shocked it was a feeling he was not to one he wasn't sure if he liked or not.

Linda didn't come, she climbed off and walked over to the mirror where she tidied herself up and checked her reflection before smoothing her skirt back down and making herself respectable again. Jez didn't say a word he couldn't believe what had just happened, not only was he now working for Linda Gerraty he had just fucked her, one of the hardest most feared ladies in London and he had just given her one although when he thought about it could that have been the other way round,? He wasn't really sure. Linda poured herself a drink and looked at Jez coldly making it plain that she had well and truly finished with him for now.

"Not a bad nights work Jez for someone so young!"

"Is that a compliment?"

"It's all your gonna get. You know me Jez; never show your cards too early! You did a good job, that bastard knows well and good that dig he just got was from me, but the ambulance, I'm not sure perhaps your too soft or you haven't the stomach for this type of work."

"Fuck off Linda you know that's not true, I just don't like playing God, he's got the message you'll get your money so what's the problem? If you're not happy though I'll carry on my own way and work elsewhere it's no skin off my nose mate, I'm only interested in the money, the sex was nice but I can do without it."

"You are one stroppy little fucker, let's just see how things go, see if you can get it right next time ah"

"Yeah yeah o.k. whatever you want Linda, you're the boss!" he grinned and although she didn't show it that grin knocked her sideways and made her breath catch in her throat.

He really was one sexy little git and he knew what he was doing, she'd definitely be having some more of that, she could still feel herself quivering for more dying to orgasm and get relief but she wouldn't allow herself to do that it would show weakness and let that child know she had an Achilles heel, she would find relief when he was gone and no one was around to witness her pleasure.

Jez left soon after and Linda was left thinking about her old friends Son. Really he was just a kid he should be pulling little tarts down the youth club finding out what sex was all about instead he'd been dragged up with it, there wasn't anything you could teach him about sex, she realised that tonight he had knowledge beyond his years both in sex and life and it didn't make her feel good. When Linda was completely honest with herself the guilt she felt in the part she played in Jez's upbringing could make her feel physically sick, she was ashamed and that was a feeling she was either used to or liked. A lesser woman might have found it too much to bear, that poor little shit had very little life outside crime, to her knowledge he'd never been on holiday, never even seen the sea. He didn't know what it was like to have a Mother who knew her job, who nurtured and fed him, who was there when he got in from School of a day who put his welfare above her own and she had played a part in that little tragedy, had kept Shirley the way she was and at the time not given Jez a second thought but things catch up with you in the end and just lately she had been thinking about her own Son. The Son that nobody except Paulie and Shirley knew existed. The Son she had given away when he was weeks old and until recently had never given a second thought. The boy that was now playing on her mind every time she looked at Jez

Chapter 14

Linda had been twenty, she'd had plenty of abortions before but she was sick of it she was sick of Doctor's, Hospitals clap clinics, she had managed to save some money and Paulie was always there to help out. Paulie was the only man who had never either paid her or forced her to have sex he had always helped her and never asked questions. Yet again she was confused, she didn't know if she wanted a baby, she didn't know who the Father was as usual she hoped it would be one of her regulars as most of them had been pretty nice to her over the years but it could be anyone's. She had to take chances most of her punters didn't like condoms, lets face it if they were not fussy they wouldn't be picking up scum like her on street corners, and fucking the life out of them or getting a sly blow job before going home to their wives and kids. If they had any respect for their families and lived decent lives they wouldn't give into their selfish urges. One thing was sure the baby wasn't Paulie's which made her sad she would have liked to have had some love in her life from a man and his child but she knew 100% it couldn't be his, they hadn't slept together in months. Paulie had been knocking off some little bird in Chelsea for a few months now and that hurt, Linda felt that a little piece of Paulie had been lost to her this time and a baby might have made all the difference, she had never been pregnant with Paulie's child otherwise an abortion would never have crossed her mind. The pain the humiliation she had gone through every time she had visited the clinic, every time the test was positive and she had agreed to be booked in immediately for the termination she didn't feel whole anymore and she was definitely harder more distant less emotional but adversely she would be back on the streets taking chances again as soon as the blood had stopped, as soon as the feeling that her guts had been ripped out stopped gnoring away at her body and soul. She knew she had been lucky she wasn't HIV positive, so many girls these days wouldn't do a double or fuck without a condom but they were the ones that could be selective and she didn't come to that category, beggars can't be choosers and she'd always been a beggar.

Once she had made the decision to keep this baby she came off the streets for a while and just enjoyed the new sensation of having something of her own growing inside her that was purely her own and no one else could take away no one else could control or infect like they had her. She loved to lay on her back feeling her bump getting bigger and bigger and imagining she could hear it's heart beat strong and clear meaning her baby was fit and healthy, for the first time in her life she began to pray, to pray to a God that up to now she had no faith in to keep her baby alive and well and her own private little prayer that it would be a boy. Boys had an easier life, boys could do what they wanted to do and she knew without a doubt she could definitely love a little boy, it worried her she might be jealous of a Daughter. A little girl who was fresh and pure a little girl who might grow up to be everything she wasn't, a little girl she was frightened she could taint and poison. What if she made her feel that all men were the same, all men used and abused women all men were vile creatures from another planet because that was often how she felt about the men she came into contact with, aliens not of this world, depraved and debauched. She didn't want a little girl to become bitter and twisted, have no respect or ambition and to accept all the shit that life can throw at you because that is how she had bought her up expecting to have a half life like her Mother.

Time was racing ahead and the birth was looming Paulie had been brilliant helping her out with money and making her life as easy as possible but he kept trying to bring her back to reality and telling her it couldn't last that she'd have to get back on the streets, that she wouldn't survive on benefits but she didn't want to listen. She had managed to stay clean since she found out she was pregnant the occasional joint or the odd drink but nothing serious nothing heavy, she had eaten well, rested and even gone for long walks, she knew she had done everything she could manage to in order to help this baby and was looking forward to the birth, she didn't want Paulie to keep trying to bring her down to earth and see reality she was enjoying the privilege of living in a little cocooned dream world for once in her life and not thinking about tomorrow. It was amazing what you could do when you are happy she'd hardly suffered at all from the drug withdrawal, she'd always tried to avoid heroin as much as possible but she had a heavy old crack habit and cannabis and brandy were also on the daily menu but she had more to think about now and as she was no longer hawking herself all over town taking any pervert with money in his pocket, her demons were letting her rest.

When the birth came it was long and painful she had been to all the anti natal classes but it still came as a shock. She was in labour for sixty hours most of it on her own and most of the time the nurses treating her like shit because of her past terminations and infections obviously they had access to her medical records and she even heard one nurse ask to be taken off her labour room roster because she was frightened of catching something and taking it home to her own children. Kindness and sympathy cannot have been part of their training and they felt they had a right to condemn and judge because they were forced to help her bring her child into her world. Paulie, God bless him kept appearing with tea, doughnuts once he even bought Shirley in but she was less than useless agitated and edgy to escape for another hit which Paulie wouldn't finance until she had made the visits. Paulie couldn't stay too long he wasn't good with things like that, didn't like the blood and gore. It had never bothered him when he was inflicting the injuries, when he was the one causing the pain but he couldn't stand all this emotion and felt helpless to help Linda get through it. The silly sod even offered her some coke when she was having some particularly bad contractions and she very nearly took it, she nearly gave in and put both her own and her unborn Childs life at risk but she stayed strong. She kept thinking about those smug patronising cunts of nurses and she wouldn't give them the satisfaction. She was determined to show them that she was strong and that she cared about this baby and that she couldn't give a fuck about what their opinion of her was.

Luke Paul came into this world on January 5th 1965 the most beautiful serene baby Linda had ever seen in her life. She gave him her favourite name but also named him after Paulie, he had always been so good to her over the years and she still regretted the fact that he was not Luke's Father. It had made him cry, the only time in her long association with him that she had even seen him close to real emotion and affection. She left Hospital and took her baby home dreaming that it was all going to be alright, that she was going to have the life that she had always wanted but it didn't take her long to realise this just wasn't going to happen. She found looking after the baby easy, he was a good little boy and although he got her out of bed twice a night, in the day he was an angel sleeping contentedly, feeding well and loved having his Mothers cuddles and kisses for hours on end but money was a problem. Linda soon realised that Paulie had been right, she couldn't cope on what the state dished out to her each week she wanted the best for her boy she wanted to be able to go out and buy him clothes, toys anything her heart desired and she couldn't. She was hardly getting enough in to pay for the nappies and milk let alone go on shopping spree's and buy luxuries for her little treasure. Paulie helped out where he could but he had his own life to live and his lifestyle didn't come cheap. She was beginning to realise that she needed to earn money and she needed to earn it fast and she knew only one way to do it, that was go back on the bash. The girl next door would look after Luke she knew that, she was as broke as Linda herself but she would never join the others on the streets, she was too timid, too straight laced but she had a couple of kids she needed to feed so she often looked after the other tom's kids or did a bit of washing and ironing, cleaning or shopping for some of the old girls on the estate just to make ends meet. So Luke was installed at number 12 every time she went out walking the streets, flogging her arse slipping back into her old life of perversion and degradation doing the things she always swore she would never do again but telling herself all the time she was doing it for Luke.

After a while Paulie set her up in a massage parlour when a big job came up trumps for him and he came into a fair sum of money so at least she was less vulnerable and working inside out of sight of the local old bill but she felt gut sick. Every time she had to ask a punter what he wanted, had to offer herself on a plate open her legs to a complete stranger, her heart fell to her boot's, she no longer had the stomach, she was a different person now, a Mother, she no longer felt her body was just her's, it was Luke's too he had grown inside her she had changed inside because of his presence for nine months and every time she let someone else in her she felt she was letting him down. All these thought's all this guilt was what led her back to the drugs, she needed to block it all out again to escape to a world where she could cope with what she was doing and carry on making money to keep Luke, but it didn't always work. The thought that she was going to lose Luke was always seeping into her mind, at night when she lay in bed, when she was shagging some sad old weirdo or even when she was in the Supermarket collecting food for the week the realisation that she was going to lose him was slowly dawning on her and it was breaking her heart. All her hopes, all her dreams where slipping away and with them her whole life was shattering in front of her eyes and there was nothing she could do about it, to survive with Like she had to work, to lose him she wasn't sure that she would survive she was caught in a no win situation that she knew she had to resolve and to do that she had to give Luke up. It was the hardest decision of her life but it was one she knew she had to make but she had to find somewhere for him where he would be safe, warm, well fed and well looked after, she had always wanted a better life for Luke she didn't want him to suffer as she had. Linda loved Luke with all her heart but she knew love wasn't enough and for his own sake she had to give him up.

Linda called the Social Worker who laughingly 'looked after' them herself and told him her decision. The bastard almost laughed down the phone at her telling her he wasn't shocked and he was waiting for her call he said she couldn't look after herself let alone a child and that his superiors should have never let her take him home from the hospital in the first place, she a filthy whore after all and once a whore always a whore. If Linda had been in the same room as the cunt she would have had no second thoughts about knifing him straight in the heart if he'd had one to knife. She knew what she was, she knew she had failed but she was doing the right thing now and what right did this wanker have to rub it in had he led a blameless life or as a sanctimonious poof was he just jealous of the amount of cock she got and he didn't, she almost told him this but she just didn't have the energy she'd lost the battle and she couldn't continue the war she was broken. Before she put the phone down he said he was arranging to have Luke picked up immediately he didn't trust her for one minute longer with her precious Son so he would be taken straight into care she couldn't answer for the tears in her eyes and the sickness in her throat as the sobs began to come.

    When she recovered slightly she went into the bedroom and packed a bag with all the things she had struggled to buy Luke in their short time together, the clothes she had lovingly washed and ironed the toys that she had bought especially for their educational value the pictures she had taken of him of Paulie of herself hoping his new Parents would give him when he was older and all that was left of her heart. When they arrived and she had to hand over the only good thing in her life to a complete stranger who arrived with the wanker who was meant to have been helping her cope making sure she was coping but in truth who had only ever bothered to turn up twice to see her they refused to take the bag. He said he wouldn't take anything from her filthy hovel to taint her child in his new life and he was sure his new Parents wouldn't want Luke to be reminded of who his Mother was or where he came from when he was older and they left. They just walked out of the door with her whole reason for living and left her in more pain and despair than she knew it was possible to feel. She was dead inside, she knew she would never as long as she lived feel the same about another human being as long as she lived and she vowed that day that she would never again have another child. Linda didn't care if she died tomorrow, she had nothing to live for so it didn't matter but if she lived to be ninety she knew that she would never carry another child to be ripped away from her by circumstances and her own weaknesses, as long as she was on this planet she would never give as much love, as much trust and as much of herself to anyone.

Her life returned to normal she sank into depression, carried on working and living life the only way she had ever known how to. The work initially was to fund her drug habit and get her through the dark days but surprisingly a steely determination to better herself began to creep into her being. She knew she would never get Luke back she also knew she couldn't go on like this feeling sorry for herself and wallowing in self pity. Linda wanted massage parlours and street corners to be a thing of the past, she wanted more she wanted better and she intended to get it.

Chapter 15

Paulie helped Linda move into the drugs trade, he had always had a finger in this pie and made a good living from it but he didn't have Linda's drive, he didn't have her ambition or the complete lack of emotion and heart. Linda had become another person, she cared for no one she worked non stop and she amassed money drugs and prostitutes like no ones business. Her life was just work and her aim was success. Linda had nothing else to live for her work was her life and for ten long years she continued to do anything for money either through drugs and prostitution empires or personally. She had hand picked her girls making sure they knew what was expected from them, she had no compassion and made them work as hard as she herself had always had to work. She was still good to them when they were in trouble or had taken a beating, she would weigh them off with a few quid until they could work again or get them a discreet Doctor to fix them up, make sure they had regular check ups with a local bent clap clinic and a minder for dodgy jobs. For all this the girls liked Linda but most of them were too stupid to realise she was only doing it for her own profit and if push came to shove she would be the first one to sell them down the river or stab them in the back. She was also getting them hooked on the drugs, the same drugs that she was supplying so Linda's was a win win situation why they were being dragged deeper into a world of degradation and pain. All and all what with her profits from the drugs, the sex and the punters spending money in her clubs her bank balance was constantly growing at an alarming rate.

Linda had to have the girls young pliant and guidable if not a bit stupid, they had to be totally in her control otherwise her operations wouldn't work and the more power she obtained the more she needed it which meant more time building her empire and more time becoming bitter and twisted and dwelling on her past and the loss of her child. Shirley had been so easy to manipulate so easy to control and Linda always gave her the worst of everything, the worst clients, the worst drugs, the worst jobs all because of her jealousy. She had a burning hatred for Shirley for one reason and one reason only and that was Jez. Shirley was poor, Shirley was weak Shirley barely existed but the one thing she had done was manage to keep her own child. Shirley hadn't been able to give Jez anything his life had been hell but she had fought tooth and nail to keep him even when he was placed in foster homes or taken into council care she fought to get him back. Whenever Jez was taken away from her, her one topic of coherent conversation would be about how she missed her boy, how she would bring him home and how much he loved her and she was right. Whatever she had done wherever she had been from the day that boy was born he had loved her, as he got older he didn't much like her but he still loved her and that love of a child for his Mother was killing Linda every time she looked at them. Linda had to give Shirley her due, she never deliberately threw it in her face that she had given Luke away never made her feel guilty but the bond between Jez and Shirley broke her heart. It was a constant reminder of the biggest mistake in her life and although she had plenty of regrets the loss of Luke was definitely the one that haunted her waking hours and would she knew for the rest of her life. All this ensured that Linda gave Shirley the hardest time she could she was well aware jealousy and bitterness were destructive emotions but she couldn't stop herself feeling them. She longed to be a proper Mother but knew now she never would. Linda had the comfort of money in the bank now a beautiful home that was all her own, she would not allow herself to have another child, she felt she deserved to be punished for her sordid and violent past, she had decreed herself unfit to carry another child and have a second chance, she couldn't bare the thought of tainting another life that she was responsible for and in her heart of hearts she knew she was right. Ultimately she didn't trust herself, didn't know if she could ever leave this life behind and be a normal person, she didn't know what a normal person was anymore and this life was her just deserts her past and her future all rolled into one.

Linda was constantly aware of what was happening to Luke she had obtained the services of a Private Investigator who made her a report every three months. Although illegal he had managed to get hold of all the details of Luke's adoption and his new Parents and through many other contacts and by becoming a Family friend himself had been able to maintain a lucrative income keeping a constant eye on Linda's precious Son and ensuring no harm came to him. The boy was safe, his new Mum and Dad had wanted kid's for years, IVF, surrogacy none of it had worked for them and at the time this had made Linda feel good, not only did she know that Luke would be very well looked after and likely to be an only child with all his new Family's love and affection lavished on him but it also gave her the feeling that she was doing something right in her life not just for Luke but for this other couple too, she had given them the ultimate gift and for the first time in her life she felt proud.

Linda waited anxiously when each report was due, the video's the pictures, later the School reports, reports of his behaviour, holidays everything that Luke done in some small way she felt she was a part of. She felt that although not physically there tainting his life she was taking part in it and doing her best for him by staying away. She would give Danny the Private Investigator extra money to buy Luke presents, Birthday's, Christmas anytime she felt she needed to feel close to him and have some control over his environment, Danny had got his own family involved, having kid's of his own it was easy for the families to make friends, spend all their time together, the kids to become best friends. Danny was so good even his Wife didn't realise she'd been set up, that the friendship that her Husband had so actively encouraged had been funded by a client.. never one to ask where the money came from as long as she could keep spending it she was very happy to holiday with her friends in France, Spain,

Skiing in Austria, the big one to Australia, she was happy as long as the money kept coming and it was a bonus she got to spend all her time with her friends. She didn't really like her Husband much and as her Children got older they grated on her nerves and had become a burden. Once the money had started coming in big time she liked her freedom, her 'me time' to sit in the beauty salon all day, spend day's at the spa, lunch with friends and the occasional afternoon's relaxation with a young, firm bodied mechanic who had started fixing her car a few months ago when she'd had a bump and had gone to pay her own bodywork as much attention as he did her 4x4. If she was honest she didn't really know how her Husband made his money but he was never at home and that suited her fine.

Luke prospered he was growing up fast and becoming somewhat notorious for his good looks among the teenage girls in the years above him. Tall for his age with dark curly hair and surprisingly startling blue eyes he was becoming very handsome. His School work was exemplary and his Teachers all commented on his ability to learn quickly whilst not exactly paying all his attentions to his studies. He was very good at sport and excelled at Football and Tennis but the worrying thing to Linda when she read his School reports was the fact that there seemed to be an underlying slight dislike of his character by his Teachers. It wasn't that he was rude disruptive or naughty but they all seemed wary of commenting on his personality. He had friends and even from a young age had been full of charm and charisma but adults didn't seem to like him much, whether that was because of cockiness, or whether it was because he had been spoiled and found it hard to relate to adults she couldn't know having no proper contact with him since he was weeks old. There was no doubt about the fact that he had been spoiled, everyone around him seemed to treat him like a little Prince, his Family, his extended Family friends and herself included through Danny, it worried her but at the end of the day there was nothing she could do about it, he wasn't her's anymore so she couldn't interfere in his life.

Things seemed to be going well, she was as happy as she could be without Luke and Paulie in her life permanently, she had her reports on Luke but Paulie popped in and out of her life whenever he felt like it and would never commit to her but he was at the end of a phone when she needed him and at times he played a large part in her work and personal life. Her work kept her busy trying to keep the girls in line and manage her empires in her quest to amass her fortune, she always made sure she was kept busy and her thoughts at work were focused and her emotions under control. She had Jez now to arm her bed when se wanted it warmed, Paulie for adult company and that was all she needed. Jez was proving invaluable as an enforcer although still only a young lad, she paid him big money to be at her side but also to salve her conscience over the way she stood back and watched the way he was treated as a child, over the way she had not stepped in and sorted Shirley out whilst all the time watching Luke every step of the way and ensuring his happiness and stability, worrying and fretting over every aspect of his life even though she hadn't seen him since he was weeks old.

Jez she saw almost every day but she had willingly stood by and watched the tragedy that was his life and not given it a second thought never bothered to make things better for him. Lately it had all began to make her feel a little uneasy so the vast amounts of money she was paying him was to help herself as much as to reward him for his services. It looked like things were set to carry on for a long time the way they were but things were definitely about to change, things were about to change for Linda in a big way and not in the way she would have hoped. Her life would never be the same again and everyone that knew her would believe that she had gone forever. Everyone that is except for Paulie whom she could never walk away from and a teenage boy making a name for himself on a council estate in Hackney.

Chapter 16

When Linda woke up that morning she could never have foreseen what was about to happen. She was due at the club at 11o'clock to see a supplier and by the time she was ready to leave it was pissing down outside. She hated the rain it bought back too many memories of standing on street corners in the old days. She got soaked getting out of the car which didn't improve her mood and when she reached the club her manager Tony hadn't opened up so she was ready to spit blood. Tony was usually reliable to the point of annoyance but today he had not phoned her and told her he would not be in so it was a bit of a shock to find the club all locked up, he knew she had an early meet so why wasn't the tosser there, she'd make sure he knew how angry she was when he turned up. As soon as she pulled out her own key's and entered the club she felt a cold trickle of fear run down her spine and an icy fist grab her heart. She knew something was wrong she just didn't know what it was yet. She switched on the over head lights Tony was nowhere to be seen but everything else looked normal everything in it's right place but that didn't make her feel any better she had expected to see a break in a mess maybe even Tony in trouble some how but everything was normal. She made her way upstairs to her office but again everything seemed normal, she felt herself shaking with nerves never a shrinking violet she didn't know why she felt so uneasy but then she opened her desk diary. It was a few minutes before she actually looked down and saw the writing scrawled across the page in thick black ink, just one word that made every hair on her body stand on end every nerve tighten, the scream trying to escape her throat freeze, just one word LUKE. What was going on here? Who was trying to frighten her? She grabbed the phone to call Paulie but just as she placed her hand on the receiver its shrill ring made her jump and the shaking started again. she lifted the handset with trepidation and waited for whoever was on the other end of the line to speak

"Yo Linda"

"Tony where the fucks are you I need you here"

"Really? I thought you didn't need anyone Linda"

"What's your problem Tony? Have you got something to say because I am in a fucking hurry!" She was trying to keep calm and stop shouting instinctively she knew Tony had something to do with this pile of shit but she couldn't work out what. Tony like everyone else knew nothing about Luke so what was going on?

"Ok ok calm down lady I am just letting you know that I've got Luke with me or sorry should I say Toby because that's what he's called now isn't it Toby Watson. Suits him better than Luke I must say. Nice kid Toby, nice Parents too much better for him than you could ever have been!"

The scream that Linda let out could have shattered crystal; she was rooted to the spot. She was trying to speak, trying to let him know what a cunt he was, what she was going to do to him when she got hold of him but at the same time her mind was working overtime. How did he know all this? How did he know that Luke even existed let alone that he was now called Toby and what he was like. Paulie and Shirley, Paulie and Shirley kept going through her head, they were the only ones, the only ones that knew about Luke she had never told anyone else even when she was full of pride for his achievements she kept it in and talked to no one except Shirley and Paulie, it had to be one of them.

"So you have someone called to Toby with you Tony who the fuck is he and what has he got to do with me?"

"Fuck off Linda I know he's your Son I know everything there is to know about it so don't try pulling my chain lady it aint going to work1"

"What do you want?"

"Money of course what else is there, although he's a good looking boy and I've always found it hard to resist a pretty face you know."

"You nonce, you dare harm a hair on his head and I swear to god I'll kill you with my bare hands, I'll hunt you down and rip your fucking head off you sick perverted bastard"

"Empty threats Linda you don't even have a clue where I am and I could use him kill him and be gone before you ever found him. Your boy could be damaged for life or even dead if I feel like it but we both know that isn't going to happen you want him back safe and sound, in one piece so stop your mouth running off with ya let's talk money."

"I've been good to you, you bastard and you treat me like this who are you working for who's paying you more money than I am, who's putting up with your shit and pulling your strings, tell me who?""You think I'm stupid, I don't need to be working for anyone Linda I have a brain of my own I'm doing this for myself, for me and Shirley, for our future"

Linda was winded she felt like all the air in her lungs had rushed out in one huge breath she lent back into the coolness of her deep buttoned red leather chair and began to feel the weightlessness of her limbs and her head began to spin not only with shock but with pure blind anger too. She knew it, she knew it couldn't be Paulie but Shirley of all people she wasn't even able to remember her own name half the time and her own Son had always faded into the back of her drug addled brain whenever she wasn't reminded he was there so how did she remember Luke and how did she know all about him now?

"If Shirley's your source then Tony you can forget it she doesn't fucking know what day it is, if she's involved you probably have the wrong kid you stupid fucker, you two together must be a fucking joke"

"Shut it Linda and fucking well listen to me now. It is your Luke we have only now he's called Toby you know that as well as I do and someone is on the way now to bring you a picture of your beloved Son so until you've seen that I suggest you stop winding me up or you may not like the consequences"

"So how much, if this is actually Luke how much do you want but remember you will never get away from me however much money you have I will track you down if it takes the rest of my life both you and that wicked piece of shit your both marked and you know it"

"Give it a rest will you, you really do think we're stupid we're not likely to hand him over to you until were well away from here, new identities, new lives it's all in place so don't try to slag me down, his fate is in your hands just remember that you stupid bitch"

"How much?"

"1 million"

"You are fucking joking"

"No Linda I'm not, you've got it you've got more than that and some, I have been keeping an eye on all your little investments and off shores so don't give me shit. Isn't he worth it?'"

"Where and when?"

"You will be told. When you get the picture you'll also get the terms and Linda, stick to them or he's gone."

The phone went dead and for a moment she was paralysed by fear. Just one word kept spinning through her head Shirley, Shirley Tony she could have expected it a chancer with half a brain and a lifestyle that needed big money, she had always been aware of his capabilities and kept to the old rules, treat him well, buy his loyalty but Shirley she had misjudged for her she should have used the other more legitimate rule of business, 'keep your friends close but your enemies closer.' Linda had always known that Shirley resented her lifestyle, her money coveted everything that she had but she couldn't have imagined in a million years that she could do this. She never thought she had the sense let alone the bottle but with Tony's help she could have just provided the info and take the money, he would have done the rest. But for betraying her Shirley would suffer more she was determined of that, she had known her too long and helped her too many times to take this shit from her. Suddenly she realised she had to move, she had to get Paulie and see what he could do, get his help to sort out this fucking mess and get it quick. Linda was panicking and panicking seriously she needed help and she needed it now.

    Paulie picked up the phone on the second ring sounding half asleep and slightly stoned.
    "Paulie get over here now I need you"
    Paulie immediately sobered up and his eyes snapped wide with concern
    "Linda what's happened?"
    "It's Luke, Tony has Luke and I need you Paulie I need help now" as she began to speak she realised her voice was getting louder and higher, she was also rocking backwards and forwards clutching her stomach feeling like her guts had been ripped out.
    "Paulie please, Paulie please"
    "Linda I'm on my way just calm down, get a drink just wait for me there I'll be twenty minutes. Linda please just calm down I will be there and we will work this out I promise"
    As he was talking he was throwing his clothes on he'd already told the little bird he'd picked up last night to fuck off and he dived into the Bathroom to splash his face and clean his teeth. It had frightened him how upset Linda was she was usually a very cool woman, nothing fazed her, nothing worried her but this was Luke we were talking about this

was different. He shot out the door and jumped in the car making his way over to the club in the lunchtime traffic his brain working overtime thinking about who he could call. Who could he trust when dealing with the kidnap of a young boy, a young boy at that who didn't live in their world who had been protected and pampered who although almost the same age as Jez but didn't have his nouse or knowledge? Jez of course that's who he'd get. By the time he'd reached the club he'd decided Jez would be the boy it would be best for the kid and for Linda to know that it was Jez who would lift the kid they would have some empathy with each other because of their age and Jez could be sympathetic when pushed. But Paulie was to get a shock when he reached Linda and she explained it was Jez's Mother who had actually set all this up, Jez's Mother who had betrayed her and Jez's Mother who was to blame for Linda's, the woman he had always loved but didn't like to admit it, distress now. Shirley would regret this for as long as she lived, if she did live of course.

Paulie poured himself a drink and prowled around Linda's office like a Panther looking for its next kill. He was trying to formulate a plan in his head. Would it be best to pull Jez in and see if he was involved or knew what he's fucking Mother was playing at or would it be best to go straight after Tony. Linda jumped when she heard a faint click down in the club; Paulie dropped his glass and took the stairs two at a time to get down to the door he had locked behind him. On the mat was a brown envelope which he tore open before he returned upstairs to Linda. His heart sank inside was an A4 sized picture of Luke and a set of instructions in Tony's distinctive scrawl telling them to bring the money to a flat in Streatham, the usual used notes, no police. How fucking stupid could they be? What did they think they were in, an old episode of the Sweeney. As if he and Linda of all people were likely to call the police, whatever was going down they would laugh in their faces for all the years of grief they'd caused them. He had to take the stuff back upstairs, he knew that but he also knew that by showing Linda that picture he was going to break her heart and crucify her all at once and it broke his own heart to have to do it, but he had no choice.

Chapter 17

Paulie went upstairs with a heavy heart, Linda hadn't moved she seemed to have become incapable of movement she was just staring into space and making clicking noises with her tongue he was getting seriously worried about the woman.

"Linda drank the brandy you need to pull yourself out of this you need to think."

"I am fucking thinking, thinking about my Son and how I've let him down about how all this is my fault about my boy Paulie"

"I know, I know Linda but I have the instructions for the money we have to decide what to do"

"We don't have to decide anything Paulie we just give them the fucking money and get my boy back"

"Linda you don't have a million here in cash, these cunts aint waiting they want it all by midnight, used notes delivered to Tony's tonight their in a hurry, their gonna think we're shitting them but you don't have that sort of ready cash we need time. What wankers thinking we can get that sort of money within twenty four hours what have they got shit for brains?"

"I have the money Paulie and what I don't have I will beg, steal or kill for; you have money how much can you weigh in until I can free up my assets?"

"Nothing like that Linda fuck me you know me money goes in one pocket and out the other all I can manage in cash is around fifty thou, where's the rest coming from?"

"I've worked it out, most of it I have in an offshore run by a client of the club, he's fucking loaded he's good for at least what I have in his bank if not a little of his own if he doesn't want his Wife getting word of what he gets up to on his little business trips to London. More than once I've had to bail him out when he's got too heavy handed with the girls keep them sweet so that he doesn't end up with a GBH conviction or going down for assault and battery. He wouldn't want his nice little Wife finding out what a pervert she's married to and there are several others who are going to learn there's always a payback I can get the money tell them we'll be there."

"That's the other thing Linda he only wants you there, the tosser as if I'm ever gonna let you walk into whatever they have going down there."

"Not your decision Paulie, not your Son just help me round up the money and I'll do the rest O,K"

"We still need back up you know that, all the way here I was thinking I'd call Jez in but that's out of the question now, it's all a bit too close to home for some of the other loud mouths and others I wouldn't want within fifty miles of a kid of mine, no fucking brains and too much temper"

"Call Jez!"

"Linda are you mad has all this scrambled your fucking brains it's the cunts Mother we are talking about here how do you know he isn't involved, he doesn't already know what's going down?"

"I don't but I intend to find out you call him now and get him in here, I'll start collecting favours and then you and he can do the pick up's. I need to keep thinking Paulie so let's just get moving and I'll work the rest out as we go along"

Paulie was far from happy when he made the call to Jez, he got on well with him, Jez was after all only a kid, a mans boy in the true sense of the word but he knew he had been shagging Linda for a while now and he didn't like the fact that Jez had never told him, he thought he was getting one over on him but of course he wasn't Paulie had known all along what had been going on. Paulie didn't want Linda all the time, she was too independent too cocky and if he were truly honest too well used for his liking, he loved her in his own way but he also liked something a bit younger and fresher in his bed. He reluctantly called Jez and asked him to come to the club he didn't want to tell him what the problem was himself he wanted Linda to do that he wasn't entirely happy about bringing him into this and he wanted to see his face when he was told his Mother was the cause of all this grief, he wanted to look into his eyes and see if he really had no idea as to what was going on. He realised Linda wanted to do the same she had known him all his life had been sleeping with him for months she would have more of an insight into his mind than he would. He went back to the flat to collect the money he had there and he went to the bank to withdraw what little he kept in a legit account, he'd arranged for Jez to be at the club in two hours so he needed to shift himself. Paulie understood that Linda must love her Son but she didn't know him, she'd had almost no contact with him for most of his life only her tame PI reports and pictures and video's, he understood she couldn't let go but her panic was something he couldn't understand. She couldn't distance herself she was too emotional having never had a child or feeling the love that exists as a parent he felt she was overreacting and as such didn't want her to do the meet. He wanted to do it himself, it wouldn't be as hard for him he could control his emotions because he felt nothing for anyone in this little scenario his only loyalty to Linda. Knowing Shirley for as many years as he had it was a sad reflection on her that he couldn't give a shit if she lived or died, as far as he was concerned she was lucky to get this far in life if he had to out her, so be it. Tony was just a wanker, a typical club barman who everyone thought was his friend but in reality he was making plans to stab them in the back, take what he could get either from the Till or on a more personal physically or mentally, he was no match but if Jez was involved that was a different matter. Jez was a cunning hard little fucker and he would have to be watched. He didn't want Linda to be blinded by their friendship and making the wrong judgements he at least needed to protect her from that.

Paulie arrived back at the club about twenty minutes before Jez was due. Linda had composed herself a little, settled her nerves with brandy made her calls, called in her favours and had a list ready and waiting for Paulie to attend to.

"How you doing babe?" he enquired as he entered her office "Any news?"

"No all quiet, I've got the money arranged I just need you to collect and get the meet sorted out I want it bought forward I want it as soon as possible, I'm not having them pulling my chain waiting around all day when I have what they wanted ready and waiting"

Paulie was shocked at the change in Linda the woman he had left had been little more than a wreck and yet here she was now calling the shots and making demands he couldn't understand what had changed. Before he could answer Jez entered the office with his usual swagger and air of confidence, Paulie clocked this and he also saw Linda's face relax a little as if she realised the kid wasn't involved., even Jez wasn't that good an actor and he would hardly have turned up as summoned if he was looking at a third share in a mil.

"Jez we have a problem" Linda stated as soon as he'd sat down and stretched his legs out looking to all and sundry like a man who had put his mark on this territory.

"Gathered that Lynn what's happening? What's so urgent I had planned to go to the match this afternoon I need a little R and R after these last few weeks your wearing me out" he said with a private smile Paulie was not meant to notice. Linda was out of her chair like a bullet out of a gun, she pulled him close to her until they were face to face no more than two inches between them. Jez didn't know what had happened and Jez was quick, Jez was usually super quick when he sensed danger but neither he or Paulie saw this coming which made it so much more frightening

"So help me God you little bastard if you don't tell me the truth I will personally cut your balls off. What do you know?"

Jez was snow white with shock, he thought she had gone bloody mad, this was all he needed some nutty old tart thinking he was up to something he wasn't, what was it with women, she knew he wasn't interested in sex as a pleasure more a necessary release of built up energy and the other bird he had fucked a few months back had been her idea, one of her new girls she wanted tried out and no one else was around he hadn't enjoyed it and they had talked about it afterwards the girl didn't even cut the mustard and he had never seen her again.

"What's the matter with you? You know I'm straight down the line what's fucking wrong here?"

"Your Mother Jeremy, your fucking Mother is what's fucking wrong now what do you know?"

"Linda you know I haven't seen her for three weeks I told you that yesterday she's either shacked up with some tosser somewhere pretending to be Pretty Woman or found some like minded vermin to get out of her tree with and poncing off them living in whatever hovel they frequent. What's she done this time then?"

"She Jeremy, has taken my Son she and that waster Tony have taken my Son and are threatening to kill him if I don't hand over a million'

"Have you gone stark bollock mad woman? One you don't have a Son and two my Mother couldn't organise a piss up in a brewery let alone a million pound kidnap, what is going on here Paulie?"

Paulie spoke for the first time.

"Jez, Linda has a Son he is almost the same age as you, she couldn't bring him up on her own so she had him adopted at two months old. She has always kept a close eye on what's been going on in his life through Danny. He's a normal kid Jez living with a normal Family until today. He's been looked after and had everything he needed until today when your Mother decided to fuck up someone else's life yet again, to interfere with what doesn't concern her and to cause more agg than she is going to know what to do with this time."

"I don't believe what your telling me here really I don't she's fucking addled you know that as much as I do"

"Yeah but somehow she's got Tony helping her. She was the only other person who knew about my Son Jez and she must have told him when she was out of it. For years she kept that secret, I paid her well to and I did what I could for you because of that but now she's got involved with that piece of shit. He's been dipping my Till and causing me grief for months but I kept him on because he was a good face to have around, good at keeping the customers sweet stopping a fight and keeping the punters in line but I know he's done this to me"

"Linda I will help you in whatever way I can, I swear I knew nothing, I hardly speak to her let alone know her secrets and her confidences but let me talk to her, let me see if I can get this sorted?"

"No I want my Son back and I want him now she can have the money but I want my Son returned to the people he knows as his Parents. I want him to know nothing of my involvement I never want him to know who his Mother really is the money means nothing I want him in one piece and untainted by their hands"

"Your call but let me come with you maybe when she see's me there she'll let the kid go, I know she hasn't got a good bone in her body but just maybe she might find one it might just work"

Paulie stood back and listened to him with hatred burning inside him if anyone were to go with Linda it should be him not some kid who'd only just learnt to wipe his own arse. He didn't want Jez taking all the glory but he couldn't say anything to Linda she had enough on her plate and she wouldn't understand. How he felt. She had made her decision and they would all have to stand by it whatever the outcome.

Chapter 18

Paulie had chosen to collect the money from Linda's contacts alone basically because he needed to get away from Jez for a while, the bloke was seriously getting on his nerves, golden boy seemed to be taking over and it was sticking in his throat. Paulie had been around for Linda for so long, he didn't think he could ever be pushed out but he was and he didn't like it. Collections complete he returned to the club to make the next step, he had not left the details and contact number for the pay off with Linda he didn't think she was thinking straight, if she called the number and started mouthing off or threatening who knew what might happen. Anyway Paulie felt that this was his part of the job and as he didn't have a lot left since Jez had muscled in and taken over. All three of them checked and rechecked the cash, they wanted no mistakes, now Paulie was back he allowed Jez to call his Mother on the number they had been given to try to find out what the fuck was going on. They switched the phone to speaker phone so that all three of them could listen to what was going on and no mistakes or misunderstandings could occur and Paulie dialled the number. Jez with the cold hand of fear gripping his heart tried to keep his composure as he waited for the only person in the world he could call blood to answer the phone and the woman sitting next to him, his friend and lover's life to either be ruined or brought back from the edge of disaster.

"Shirley, how you doing"

"Good baby how did you know I was here?"

"How do you think I know Mother did you not realise that you and your little game would bring trouble to my door, did you not think that the first person they thought was involved with this shit would be me? Are you really that fucking stupid woman?"

"Why would you be involved? After all you have been giving the woman one for months now, did you think I didn't know? Did you think I was really that stupid?"

"What the fuck has that got to do with all this? Why would you care who I'm doing? Let's face it many's the time you would have sold me to a punter man or woman if the price had been high enough for your next fix, many the time you have made me watch you with whoever had a few bob in his pocket to pay for a fuck with a little extra kick, an audience or a video, so what business is it of yours and don't you dare you use me as an excuse you sick bastard"

"I've done wrong, I know that I have never pretended to be an angel but I have had enough, I can't take anymore, I want to give it all up and go away but for that I need money big money. Tony said this would be the quickest way to do it and that we could go away together and start again, make a new life and leave all this behind. We need a fresh start and we deserve it really Jez we do "

"I don't fucking believe you woman, do you actually think that piece of shit will spend the rest of his life with you? He doesn't care about any woman let alone a drug wasted old whore like you, he prefers men to women anyway you stupid bitch did you not realise he's an old queen. All he wanted from you was Linda's secrets so that he can get hold of her money. You fucking waste of space. He really knew how to get you didn't he, what's he been doing? Supplying the coke, the brandy shagging what's left of your brains out and telling you he loves you at the same time, what is wrong with you woman. You of all people have had enough men to know what's what, let the kid go. I'll help you with money, help you get away but don't cross Linda Mother and whatever you do don't hurt that kid that would not only be the end of you it would be the end of me to. Please take him home, forget about the money we will sort it out"

"No Jez this is my last chance, this is what I want, you've made your own life now Jez and you chose Linda. She has taken everything from me since the day I met her and now she's even got you, now it's my turn to take something back, at least I haven't screwed her little boy like she's screwing you. You can look after yourself,"

"I've always had to look after myself I never had a choice did I you selfish old witch. I will never forgive you for this, don't ever come looking for me, don't ever ask for my help because I am gone from your life today if you do this"

"Where are you Jez? Are you with her, is that why your saying these things? She made me what I am can't you see that, she got me on the game, sucked me into the drugs, kept me poor, kept me working cant you see that? Tony made me see that"

"I will kill that cunt, you tell him he's a dead man from today onwards I will make it my mission in life to disembowel the wanker for bringing this lot down on my head"

Linda could stand it no longer she cut in before this touching little Mother and Son chat got out of hand and demanded to know what time she could deliver the money. Shirley was frightened as soon as she heard Linda's voice, you could tell by the quiver in her words, with her Son her emotions had been pouring out with Linda she was guarded, her sentences short, her words clipped she just wanted to be off the phone and get the money in her hands. Jez suddenly realised that his Mother was petrified of Linda and probably always had been. He realised that a little part of what his Mother said about her lifestyle probably was quiet true, Linda did control people, did make their lives a misery and did use everyone for what she could get but he pushed the thought to the back of his mind. He couldn't let them invade his thoughts at the moment, couldn't show that he was weakening to his own Mothers unhappiness and way of reasoning. He had to stay strong until all this was over and then he could let pity for his Mother seep into his soul but not yet. He had to save her from herself so he had to keep the contempt he had always felt for her at the front of his mind. For years afterwards those thoughts and feelings would haunt him from that day when the whole of his life would change and the part he played in his Mothers downfall would shape his whole future.

Shirley's greed got the better of her and she had agreed they could bring the money over straight away. Linda had realised by now that Tony wasn't there where he was she didn't know but she could guess that he wanted to be out of the way in case of trouble so he'd left Shirley to accept the money and take any nasty consequences that might be attached. Tony didn't have Luke which was the main concern, Linda could hear Top of The Pops in the background and she was pretty sure that wouldn't be either Shirley's or Tony's taste. She was also sure she could hear teenage voices both male and female and both Paulie and Jez had agreed with this when she voiced her suspicions. Shirley had said Jez could come with Linda believing in her heart that he would never harm his own Mother and hoping that he may even be her saviour if Linda kicked off. She couldn't believe that if push come to shove he would abandon her even though he was angry with her now, she needed to believe that he would still protect her and still love her that was all she had left. On Jez's part he believed Linda was going to hand over the money make sure her Son got home safely, which was his job and let Shirley walk away, for now that was. He wasn't stupid enough to believe there would be no reprisals but he did believe that they wouldn't come today, he thought Linda would take no chances with what was obviously a precious Son and that she put faith in the fact that revenge was best served cold. He knew without doubt there would be a comeback but he thought he had time to think about it, he did not think the backlash would be instant.

Tony's flat was just like any other situated in a filthy tower block sink estate in South London. Linda was quiet shocked at the shitty area he lived in, she paid him well and along with what he creamed off the top she thought he could have afforded better than this but people never stop surprising you. She had once known a girl who was piss poor and lived in a block like this but then she found out she had attended Rodean and Daddy was a high court judge but her Father wanted her to become a high class madam when she graduated and supply clients for both himself and his friends. She refused so he cut her off without a penny and she ended up servicing clients from a dingy flat on a council estate but she preferred to do that than provide Tom's for her own Father. Funny how a sick barstard like that could breed a woman of principle. They reached the flat and Shirley opened the door looking pale and drawn, the background noise had now stopped. you could see Shirley was out of her head and Jez pushed passed her without a word to see if anyone was in the flat. When he reached the second bedroom and looked in there was a dark haired boy in bed with what was very obviously a much older tom, when he saw the track marks on her arms he froze with fear, if Linda found out her Son had just shagged a drug addicted whore, by the looks of things without a condom his Mother would be stone dead. He shut the door behind him and walked over to the bed, the tom was less out of it than Luke and she reached out to extend an invitation for him to join them by grabbing his crotch. Like lightening Jez twisted her arm back around behind her back and placed his other hand over her mouth so she couldn't scream out in pain.

'Listen to me and listen to me properly. Do you know who is out in that living room I'll tell you shall I it's Linda Gerraty and you have just shagged her teenage Son. Do you know what she will do to you if she finds out? I'll tell you again shall I? It will be your last day on this Earth and you won't leave it with a whimper trust me'

The woman's eyes had snapped open wide with fear at the mention of Linda's name and she was now shaking uncontrollably.

'Now I suggest you get dressed and get out on that balcony before I throw you out of the fucking window as an act of mercy because if she finds you here you will suffer believe me you will suffer. Now you have seen nothing and heard nothing and stay on that balcony until either that arsehole of a Mother of mine let's you in or you freeze to fucking death understood. Before you ask, no you aint getting fucking paid and if you've given that kid anything you better hope it kills you before she finds you.'

He left the room and returned to the hall where Linda and Shirley were standing ten feet apart, Linda's disgust and temper hardly held in check but she knew she had to make sure Luke was there before she acted. Jez positioned himself between them before he informed Linda that Luke was in the bedroom but out of it.

"You piece of shit Shirley you gave my boy gear"

"Your boy has been coming to me for weeks buying gear Linda you just never got to hear about it."

Linda's face was less animated now her expression frozen in a mask of hatred.

"Take him Jez"

"I'll wait for you Linda"

"Jez I said take him home, get him as far away from here as possible, I will give Shirley the money we'll sort something out." her voice dripped with venom

"Linda please you'll need a car, Luke's not going to wake up yet he's to out of it let's just all leave together"

"Jez why do you just not do as I ask?" as she said this Linda covered the ground between herself and Shirley with breakneck speed, Jez had not noticed before that she was holding a small vial in her right hand, she threw the contents of the vial at Shirley's face. Shirley's skin began to literally melt, bits began to fall off after they had bubbled shrivelled up and died, clumps of hair were on the carpet, her eye's seemed to be popping out of their sockets. At first she didn't scream and Jez couldn't move. It was like watching the wicked witch of the East disintegrate in the Wizard of Oz film he'd watched when he was a kid. Shirley had dropped to her knees on the floor, he realised the reason she wasn't screaming was that her throat was open to the air, hissing out of her windpipe. Her neck and chest were like a piece of raw meat. Jez could hear himself begging with Linda who had just gone crazy punching, hitting, kicking the woman that lay on the floor in front of her, the blood splattering the walls, her skull open to her Sons horrified eye's. He finally sprang into action and pounced on Linda; trying to hold her back but her strength seemed super human he had never seen her like this before. The bile rose in his throat and burnt his mouth and tongue as he began to vomit violently besides his Mothers body. His only thoughts were how to stop Linda from killing his

Mother but in years to come he often thought it might have been better if she had.

He was never sure where Paulie appeared from, he must have been close by. The first he was aware of him was when he saw him carrying Luke, still knocked out, over his shoulder and out of the flat. Linda had already disappeared and his Mothers body lay inert on the floor next to him. He realised he must have passed out for a few minutes but all he could hear now was a distant scream, for a second he hoped it was his Mother, at least that would mean she was still alive but then he realised it was the girl on the balcony who had witnessed it all and was in deep shock. He grabbed his mobile and called an ambulance, he was pretty sure his Mother was still alive, just and then he walked away from the flat. What else could he do, if she were no longer for this world then so be it but he had to watch his own back now and make sure that Linda knew he had not betrayed her. That was the way his world worked.

Chapter 19

Jez didn't really know where to go or what to do. He knew that it would be only a matter of time before the Police came to tell him about his Mother so in the end he went home. As he let himself into the flat he realised someone else was already there, the hairs on the back of his neck stood to attention and the adrenaline kicked in but the logical part of his brain told him it would be Paulie. He was sitting on Jez's sofa with a cup of tea in his hand as if nothing had happened.

"How is the old girl?"

"How the fuck do I know, how the hell could I stick around for help after what that bitch done to her, what would I tell the old bill when they turned up?"

"What happened there for fuck's sake, she seemed sane when we left here she seemed like she was going to do the right thing, hand over the money, get the kid back and sort it all out later. I could not believe the fucking scene when I walked in that place and now she's gone on the missing list."

"She's done what?"

"I took her home before I dropped the kid off on his Parents doorstep, happy they were not but I said I had found him in the street and looked in his wallet for I.D, he still didn't know what day it was so he wasn't saying any different but I don't know what he had been given to be so out of it to miss all that."

Jez sat down on the sofa opposite Paulie and put his head in his hands. Paulie actually felt sorry for him for a second, he was after all only a kid himself and he had just witnessed the destruction of his own Mother, however much of a cunt she was she was still blood and the only blood this kid had

The knock at the door made them both jump and they both instinctively knew it would be the Police. Jez went to the door with a heavy heart and let them in. Over the years they had visited this flat so many times they had lost count, they knew Jez well and they also knew Paulie, neither of these two had ever caused them much trouble it was their associates they were always lifting. They also felt sorry for Jez, he'd had a shit life so far and they now had to inform him his Mother was in a coma unexpected to survive in the Whittington on life support. These two hadn't gone to the Hospital to try and find out who the Woman was and try to sort things out, it had been a younger colleague who had drawn the short straw and it had become common knowledge that he had vomited all over the floor of the Intensive Care Unit floor when he had seen what was almost a piece of raw living flesh in the bed. No one deserved that fate, no one should survive to suffer that much pain whatever they had done in their lives that was just too much. After they had told Jez all they knew they left telling him they would return as soon as they had anymore information about what had actually happened and if there were any faces in the frame. They had offered him a lift to the Hospital to see his Mother but he had refused, he said Paulie would take him in and that if he heard anything himself or Shirley regained consciousness he would let them know. Paulie heaved a sigh of relief, at least she wasn't dead, at least Linda couldn't be charged with murder if ever anyone decided to inform on her but he had to make sure that Jez wouldn't talk. He had already gone back to the flat and sorted the girl on the balcony when he had seen Jez leave the flat and before the Ambulance had arrived She was telling no one nothing and getting on the first flight to Amsterdam in the morning. She was heading for one of his friends brothels over there with a pocket full of his money and a case full of smack. She would be happy and forget she ever saw anything, her head was so fucked up that in a couple of day's she'd think she had dreamt it anyway but if she hadn't O D on the smack she would be sorted in a couple of weeks, she wasn't a loose end he intended to leave hanging.

"Jez you know this has got to be kept quiet at any cost don't you?"

"Do I look stupid Paulie? I am gutted I have just watched my own Mother near on murdered but stupid I'm not. I still have to live and work I don't intend to fuck up like Shirley did and I definitely don't intend to upset Linda. My future is what I'm looking at now, can't look back you have no worries its safe. It has to be."

"O.k. mate I had to ask you know that don't you. At the end of the day I can't let your mouth run wild and jeopardise Linda's freedom, sorry but that's the way it goes."

"No problem!"

Jez went to the Hospital later that day and couldn't believe the sight of his Mother as she lay in the bed. The coppers had warned him she wasn't a pretty sight but as he looked at her with tubes coming out of every orifice she was unrecognisable as the woman who had brought him into this World. In all honesty there was no point in him being there. Shirley couldn't see him, couldn't talk to him and the Doctor's were not even sure if she could hear him but he sat by her bed holding her one good hand, virtually the only part of her body that had not been burnt or broken and whispered for hours how sorry he was, how sorry that he had stood by and watched this happen, that he hadn't been able to protect her and that he loved her. The Nurses just thought they were witnessing a normal reaction of a Son who had not been around when his Mother had run into trouble and needed him most, when something so vile had happened to her and he felt so helpless and guilty but of course that wasn't the case. Jez was sorry he had been there, Jez was sorry he'd witnessed it all and Jez was sorry he hadn't lifted a finger to help her. But worst of all Jez was horrified by his own lack of loyalty to his Mother and his promise to keep Linda out of the arms of justice.

For a few months things went back to normal, Linda reappeared having covered her tracks meticulously and removing herself from any suspicion of her presence at the scene. The Police could find no evidence at the scene, Shirley although now awake was unable to communicate or even think for herself and Tony had never been seen again. Jez was back in Linda's bed which even shocked Paulie and both the incident and Linda's Son where never mentioned again. Life had gone back to how it was before the shit hit the fan; the club's the drugs' the enforcing it was just as if nothing had ever happened. Then one night when Linda was at home alone a fire broke out when a cigarette was dropped on a mattress. Neighbours called the Fire Brigade and the body of a woman believed to be in her late thirties, early forties was found in the bedroom. The body was so badly burned she was unrecognisable and has Linda had never visited a legit Dentist there were no records to check against the body which the Police suspected to be her. The Coroner returned a verdict of accidental death saying he believed the body to be that of Linda Gerraty and the case was closed. To all intents and purposes everyone believed it had just been a tragic accident except Jez. Jez knew in his Heart that the woman who had caused such pain and suffering to his own Mother still walked this Earth. He also knew that one day their paths would cross again because he would make certain of it, he would make sure that he had his chance to exact his revenge on Linda for his Mother's attack and he would mete out the revenge she would never be able to mete out herself. Jez may have spent the last few months back in Linda's bed, continuing to be her henchman and shagging her brains out whenever she clicked her fingers but she had badly underestimated him, he had no intention of letting her get off Scot free and if she now thought by faking her own death she would escape his retribution she had another think coming

Jez knew Linda had to get out, had to lay low and get away from the mess she had caused, to start again in a new life. Things had not been the same since everyone knew Linda had a weakness, other firms had tried to take what was her's, she had lost business and most of all she'd lost face. Even the girls had started to treat her differently and she had in an unguarded moment admitted to Jez that she didn't have the enthusiasm anymore to pull them in line and get them sorted. Linda had made her money and in a funny way got the notoriety and reputation she had always craved. Her lifestyle had nearly got her Son killed and she wouldn't take that chance again. She had told Jez that she wanted to slow up pull back, keep her interests but take a less active role but Jez knew as well as she did that would never happen. It wasn't possible in this World, if you're a face, that face needs to be seen out and about not sat at home watching Eastenders on the box, keeping up the image and the pressure on your rivals had to be constant or you would sink. Linda had made her exit the only way she could and she obviously didn't intend to let Jez in on the deception or her whereabouts in her new life. Paulie would know where Linda was Jez knew that but he would never, not even on pain of death let on as to her location. The guy was in love with her only he didn't know it himself, he would put Linda's life above his own so there was no point even going down that dead end. For now Jez would have to move on and make his own way in life but he would never lose sight of the revenge he needed to soothe his soul. He could never forgive himself for letting his Mother down and he would never rest in peace if he didn't put this wrong right.

Over the years Jez stayed in the club trade but stayed away from the drugs. He had changed, he no longer wanted to mix with those kinds of people and he moved more into management and security but after ten years he was getting sick of it. Jez didn't have a home to go to at night, he owned a house but it wasn't a home. He had continued over the years to take sex only when he needed it, no emotion no attachment just a fuck and goodbye and he was basically still happy like that but he wanted a home. Jez wanted to make his proper mark on his house, spend some time there, learn some DIY become a typical middle aged bachelor, be proud of his home and maybe in the future really settle down and become a normal human being. This all spurred him on to leave the clubs behind and whilst he was pondering his future he had met the woman he thought could change his life for the better. Pandora Green

Pandora had come into the club one day to meet up with another girl she was hoping to sign up for her modelling agency. Jez got chatting to Pandora whilst she sat at the bar waiting for the girl to arrive he realised that she was the first woman that had really interested him for a long, long time. In the end Pandora had her meet with the model and business done returned to the bar and stayed chatting to Jez all night until closing time. He knew she was offering herself openly to him but it wasn't that Jez was interested in. he wanted to go and work for Pandora. She had told him she needed help keeping the agency going, both on the muscle side when some sick bastards couldn't distinguish between fantasy and reality and started pestering or stalking the girls and on the day to day management side. Pandora had admitted she wasn't a stayer, she wasn't prone to stick at things long but the money the agency pulled in was fantastic and she didn't really want to lose that income but she had other things she wanted to do. Jez saw his chance. He liked Pandora, thought he could work well with her, he had the skills that she needed especially on the muscle side of things but he didn't like to be too tied down. He told Pandora he might be interested if she were serious about getting someone in but that he needed to run things his own way. He couldn't run on rules and regulations he would need a free hand. Having listened to him Pandora said that if she decided to run with her own plans she would get back in touch with him.

Jez heard nothing for almost six months and had almost forgotten the conversation he had with the stunning spiky bird until she walked back into the club. Jez had already put his departure in motion so it seemed like fate when Pandora turned up again and he grabbed the opportunity with both hands and jumped into the modelling world without a backward glance. He liked what he did, liked most of the girls, the only thing that made him slightly uncomfortable was Pandora's blatant desire to bed him. She was not used to being turned down and didn't take it too well most of the time especially as Jez had slept with a couple of the other girls on occasion. Pandora didn't know that Jez would never sleep with her because he actually liked her which was against his own code of conduct, she was tasting rejection for the first time and she couldn't bare it. This said it didn't really ruin their working relationship and they continued to get on well and make a lot of money in the process so they were both happy.

When Pandora finally told Jez she was going to take a step even further away from the agency and set up her decoying business he was disappointed but not surprised. He knew she was restless but he had to admit he wished she would choose to do something a little less dangerous. Jez had known Pandora long enough now to know she would do exactly what she wanted when she wanted and no one else would change her mind for her. Jez knew her little friend Louise had already read her the riot act and told her she didn't like it but Pandora had dug her heels in and they had nearly fallen out big time over what Pandora saw as interference. Jez would keep stumm, be watchful, take an interest look out for her safety but say nothing about her decision to start her new venture, he liked her too much and didn't want to chance losing her friendship for good by rocking the boat.

Chapter 20

The decoy agency had been set up and things started a bit slow. Pandora spent a lot of time popping into the model agency mainly because she was bored but also because she enjoyed her chat's with Jez and the girls if any of them were around. it had become a sort of social club where they would all sit around drinking coffee and chatting. When Pandora got her first assignment she was over the moon and Jez was the first person she wanted to tell. she arranged to meet Jez for lunch one day and over the starter's told him of a Woman called Janelle Anstruthers who had married a much younger man and who she was sure had cheated on her on more than one occasion and was now having a fairly intense affair. Jez begged her to be careful, warned her not to get too involved but made no further comment. When pan had decided on this course of employment he had already made his mind up to make it his business to find out as much about her clients as possible but he didn't feel it was necessary to let Pandora know of his intentions. Pandora was on a high, she couldn't wait to get started and told Jez that Louise was going with her to meet the client and get the background information she needed.

Jez had no contacts in the part of surrey where this woman lived so he was pleased Lou was going with pandora, he believed in safety in numbers where woman were concerned and he trusted Lou's judgement, good sense and discretion. he had often relied on Lou's opinion when he had to call her in the past because pandora had thrown a hissy fit or made an unsound decision and Lou would step in as mediator or the voice of good sense. Louise had her head on straight; he would get in touch after the meet and see what her take on it was. pandora thought she was streetwise but decoying was a dodgy business and she could be headstrong, get herself in too deep, he was also well aware that she couldn't keep her knickers on and that sort of behaviour was likely to bring her grief in this sort of game. Women were feral where this sort of thing was concerned you couldn't take one woman's money to uncover her husband's infidelity and be the one he was being unfaithful with without getting yourself into hot water. He worried about Pandora's lack of morality and the fact that she could never see she was doing wrong where sex was concerned, Jez had spent most of his life around that sort of behaviour and knew first hand the consequences that the lifestyle could bring.

Jez called Louise and found out more about the intriguing Janelle Ansthruthers. He had already made some enquiries, getting in touch with long past contacts, searching the internet and taking a trip down to Wentworth to get a look at the house, but he wasn't getting far, he kept hitting a brick wall. Jazz was getting very uneasy and some of the old feelings of apprehension and fear that he thought he had left in his past started to resurface and he couldn't put his finger on why. His instinct told him he needed to get a look at this Janelle but he knew Pandora would never allow him to go to the next meet with her. He knew he had to watch all their backs. What had made him most uneasy was the way that when he questioned Louise she had made a very unflattering judgement of the woman. Lou wasn't usually quick to judge people, he had never heard her slag anyone off or put anyone down before, when he had first met her was shocked that she was such a good friend of Pandora's they were so like chalk and cheese. But he had to admit he had been further shocked a few weeks ago when Pandora let slip that Lou was having an affair with a bloke she had met through her. Louise was so normal, so straight and her old man was a diamond, solid dependable and he very obviously adored Louise, so what the fuck was she doing going behind his back. it had changed his view of her personally but he still knew she had Pandora's welfare at heart and Louise seemed to have made the decision on their first meeting that she did not like this Janelle woman at all. Louise had said the woman had an attitude, was downright rude and seemed to have a core of steel being devoid of any emotion whilst discussing her husband's infidelities. it worried Louise that when she spoke of Rory she showed no compassion just a burning desire to know if he were making a fool of her, not by his infidelities but by the continuation of an affair that she felt could threaten her standing in the community and cause her to loose face.

Lou's mistrust had transferred itself to Jez and his mind skipped back almost twenty years and the one person who he had tried to bury at the back of his mind for so long, the one name that kept forcing itself to the front of his brain and screaming at him and that name was Linda Gerraty. Jez kept telling himself he was being stupid, that Linda couldn't be the only woman to display these strange traits but the thought wouldn't go away it just kept picking at his brain and making his stomach turn, he had to see Janelle and put his own mind to rest, had to make sure that his mind was not playing tricks on him and making him paranoid otherwise he would never rest. Jez had grilled Lou extensively as to Janelle's looks but of course he knew that Linda would have had to change her appearance in order to have changed her life, but he was sure if he could get close enough to look her in the eye he would know for sure. Jez was sure if he could see Janelle Ansthruthers close up he would know if she was the woman he had a hatred growing like a cancer inside him for so many years, burning him up with hatred and growing with intensity every time he thought of her and what she did but how could he get close to the woman without letting Pandora think he was checking up on her or telling her about his past life. Jez was fiercely protective of his private life and especially his past and although he loved Pandora he could not trust her not to endanger herself with this woman or keep a secret. he had to think logically and decide what to do, if Janelle Ansthruthers really where Linda Gerraty he had no intention of letting this drop and he didn't want Pandora within a million miles of her. Lou had said this Janelle woman had seemed respectable a leopard didn't change it's spots and for all her bravado and imagined worldliness Pandora would be no match for Linda but Jez was a different matter. Linda wouldn't get away from him this time. he had lost her once and failed to avenge his Mother for the nightmare inflicted on her deliberately by this piece of shit and it wouldn't happen again. Jez had to make a visit and he knew it would have to be soon.

In the meantime, Pandora had been carrying on oblivious to all this going on in Jez's mind. She was preparing to meet Rory and was very happy that he was so good looking and according to his wife, charming, witty and obsessed with sex. Rory sounded just like her kind of man and along with the pleasure she thought she would gain from this job she was excited at the thought of making herself a name as a decoy. Pandora was well aware that certain people thought she was bubble headed and stupid but she knew she could look after herself, couldn't they see that after being bought up by woman like Carrie you learnt how to be streetwise and look after yourself. she often preferred to be seen as someone who needed to be Mothered and looked after but basically that was just for show, she was capable of looking after herself and more than capable of getting herself out of sticky situations with a man. Lets face it she had plenty of experience with men and their peccadilloes. This Rory wasn't going to change her life, or so she thought.

Jez was looking for a way to get a look at Janelle without her getting sight of him yet. he knew she would recognise him immediately and he would be at a disadvantage because at the end of the day he still didn't actually know if this really was Linda or if his gut feelings had let him down for the first time in his life. he couldn't exactly ask Pandora for a picture of her first client and he wasn't about to resort to hanging around outside her house wearing a trench coat and dark glasses, there had to be another way. This dilemma was causing him to spend a lot of time and energy on a solution when the devastating news hit him that his Mother had died. He had always continued to visit her, made sure she was comfortable and made sure she had everything that she needed and although theirs had never been a loving Mother and Son relationship over the years of her confinement and vegetation his childhood type of love for her had returned in a strange sort of way although he was now the adult influence and she the child like Woman. Her death at a time when he sensed Linda had resurfaced in his life was like a sign from God, a sign from a God that he had been right all along and that he must find Linda and punish her for Shirley's years of agony and subsequent early death. Jez was beginning to realise he would need help but he knew he would have to be careful who he asked for it. The only contacts Jez still cultivated were unfortunately also Paulie's and Jez was sure that wherever Linda was, Paulie would still be her confidante. Jez was one hundred per cent sure that Paulie was the only person who knew where Linda had disappeared to and what she had been doing but Jez also knew he would never tell him even on pain of death. He knew that particular door would most definitely be shut in his face and the aftermath of the two men clashing wouldn't benefit anybody so he had to find another way in to Janelle Anstruthers inner circle.

Jez was still trying to work all this through his mind, he had waited years for this opportunity and he didn't intend to jump in feet first and ruin what might be his last chance to ease his conscience and bring some peace into his life. Linda may have changed her appearance but he hadn't and he didn't want her to know that he was a friend and associate of Pandora's, he would never put her life in danger and he knew that if this was Linda and she realised who Pandora's partner was she would be dead. The answer to Jez's problem came from an unexpected quarter in the form of Lou. Jez knew of her affair with a guy she had met through pan but when she turned up with him at Jez's office one day on their way out to lunch to deliver some advertising Pandora had asked her to arrange Jez felt like he had been hit with a baseball bat. There standing in front of him was a tall dark haired man with piercing blue eyes and a cockiness that proved he was completely sure of himself and the fact that he had a fatal attraction to Women. Jez immediately took a dislike to him, the blood in his veins turning to ice, his heart pumping out of his chest, every muscle in his face pulled as tight as a bow string as the man put out his hand to greet him. Jez couldn't move, he was totally immobile rooted to the spot the colour draining away from his face. Lou took a step backwards, she actually thought that Jez was going to leap forward and rip Toby apart and her confusion over Jez's reaction was making her brain fuddled and her movements slow. She had never imagined that Jez could behave like this. Lou was always aware that Jez would not like the fact that she was having an affair, even though it was none of his business Jez was always so protective and supportive of everyone involved with the agency, she expected tight lips and a bollocking in private after she had bought Toby to the office but not this. For God's sake she hadn't even decided if she was going to stay with Wayne or leave with Toby as he had asked yet and for someone like Jez who wasn't even related to get so pious really got her back up. She liked Jez he was important to her but she didn't like the way he had just behaved, she felt he had acting appallingly on a first meeting with a friend of hers and she was just regaining her composure enough to tell him how unhappy she was when he seemed to snap out of whatever was concerning him and reached out his hand to take Toby's but it was all a bit late, it had already been noted by Toby.

Jez's mind was spinning, he had realised as soon as the man walked into the room that he had met him before, he knew their paths had crossed many years ago that fateful night when what he knew as his Mother was replaced by a vegetable. he knew without a shadow of a doubt that this was the man that had unwittingly turned Linda into the uncontrollable monster that had changed all their lives forever. This was Linda Gerraty's son. Without a shadow of a doubt Jez knew that this cunt shared Linda Gerraty's blood and all of a sudden he realised the door he had been searching for, for nearly twenty years had just swung open like the door to Aladdin's cave magically in front of his own eyes. Jez suddenly felt ecstatic, he could finally believe that he would have the chance to lay all his own ghosts to rest but he had to keep calm and make sure he didn't show his hand too early. A mantra had popped into his head and he realised he was repeating it over and over in the dark corners of his mind, 'she will suffer, she will suffer was all that he could think about and now he knew it would not be long before she did.

Jez managed to continue to make small talk with Toby for a few more minutes before the words began to stick in his throat, all he really wanted to do was get Lou and Toby out of the office so that he could sit and think. He could see Lou was annoyed with him for the reaction he had displayed when she had introduced Toby, but that was tough he'd have to square it with her later. he reminded himself that he didn't owe her anything, didn't have any loyalty to her and anyway he was just beginning to realise sweet little Lou was just like most other Women and only thought of themselves. What was she doing doing flaunting her latest fuck around friends and family whilst she was still married to Wayne, his heart went out to the poor bloke who obviously had no idea what his slag of a wife was up to while he was knocking his bollocks off at work trying to get them a better life. Sometimes poor sod's like that could make you weep they were so trusting and decent and it caused a tightness in his chest when he thought of his reaction when he found out what she had been up to and he would, they always did. He really couldn't give a shit what Lou thought of him now but it made him sick to realise he would have to keep her sweet if he was to get close to Toby and find out what he knew of his background, his adoption and whether he knew who and more importantly where his real Mother was. Jez had to be sure, he had to make certain that this really was Luke Gerraty and work out how he could use him to get to that piece of shit that bought him into the world. As much as it made him baulk Jez realised that he was going to have to make a huge effort to meet Toby socially and pretend to enjoy his company, he would also have to pretend to Lou that he was happy accepting their relationship in order to find out what she knew about this pratt. He couldn't just jump in and ask the sort of questions he needed answered otherwise one of them might smell a rat and realise something was wrong, he would have to reign himself in and bide his time. Jez knew first hand how dangerous Linda could be; she had almost destroyed him through his Mother from the day he was born but now the tables where turning and she would be the one destroyed by her own actions.

Chapter 21

Jez was getting frustrated, it had been two months now and although he had spent far too much time for his own liking with Lou and Toby he wasn't getting the answers he wanted from the smarmy bastard. Jez remembered that a large part of the problem back when the kidnap had taken place was that Luke had been heavily into drugs as a teenager that was how Shirley had been able to wheedle her way into his life and become his friend and pusher. That had been Shirley's way of hurting Linda and setting off the disastrous chain of events that were to follow the kidnap. Jez was one hundred percent sure that Toby was still using drugs but more discreetly than in the past but Lou the poor naive fucking idiot was totally oblivious to his other activities she was so besotted with the cunt and in some ways so bloody innocent she couldn't see what was right under her nose. But Jez with all his years of experience in the drug trade was sure he knew what he was about, knew all the signs but when he had once tried to brooch the subject with Lou she didn't want to know she wanted to close her ears and bury her head in the sand she was not prepared to take any criticism of this new man and got upset which jeopardised Jez's chances of obtaining the information he wanted so he had been forced to drop the issue and pretend that maybe he had been wrong all along. Her marriage was in tatters although he was pretty sure that Wayne was in the dark about her affair with Toby and Jez was hoping it would stay that way. Wayne was far too good a bloke to get hurt in that way but at the same time he felt sorry for the poor fucker being deceived and cheated on by that little tart of a wife of his. Calling Louise Carter a tart was the last thing Jez would have imagined a few months ago but now his feelings ran so deep about her betrayal of her Husband it was how he thought of her. Jez could see Lou was totally besotted by this bloke and that was another thing that convinced him he was Linda's Son. He could still recall the sly cunning charm of the man when he was just a boy and wanted to wriggle out of anything he didn't like, he had been pampered and spoiled by his adoptive Parents and Linda secretly from a distance and now Toby was showing all these traits which although he found abhorrent seemed to be a fatal attraction for Lou. Jez decided the only way he was going to find out the information he wanted on this man and his Mother was to play along with the friendship deception and keep his eye's and ears open at all times. After all Jez had one major advantage and that was that he was never out of his box, he was accomplished at pretending he was, had used this skill often enough in the past to get what he wanted and he would bet his house on the fact that Toby spent most of his time in a cocaine haze, he just couldn't understand how an intelligent girl like Louise hadn't caught on to it yet.

But at the end of the day that wasn't his problem it was his advantage, Lou would have to look after herself.

Over the months Jez had managed to glean that Toby knew he had been adopted but denied any knowledge of his birth Parents. He said he remembered presents, holidays and affection from a man called Danny who had a family of his own but spent a lot of time with him. He said as a kid he had always wondered if Danny were his real Dad because he always paid him so much attention and wanted to know everything he did. He also said that he remembered his Parents getting regular windfalls of money which allowed them to maintain their comfortable middle class lifestyle, posh Hotels, lavish holidays and even stay in their smart expensive home after his Father had died an untimely death due to a heart attack when he was only fifty three but he said he never knew where the money came from. Jez got the impression that Toby would never care where money came from as long as it came, he hadn't seemed to worry about the fact that his Mother had lost her Husband, the love of her life and her only reason for living was Toby as long as they were still comfortable financially. It didn't seem to matter to him that the only Father he had ever known had left his life as long as he still had his home comforts which Jez would never understand. With his own background and everything that had happened between him and his Mother he still mourned her loss, still missed her in his life almost everyday. Jez began to pick away at Toby as if he were a sore a festering wound he couldn't leave to heal asking well planned questions and locking any titbits of information away in his vault like brain.

He wanted the whole picture before he made his move, he intended to make no mistakes and wanted to make sure Linda suffered as much as his Mother had through the only thing that Linda Gerraty had ever loved and treasured, her Son Luke who was now Toby. She may call herself Janelle, she may have made a new life and left her sordid unpleasant past behind but he would guarantee she would never leave her son behind completely that she must know of his whereabouts his life, still be interfering and supporting him from a distance. As long as Linda lived Jez knew she would still know all she possibly could about her precious boy, making sure he got all he wished from life and watching his back. This understood Jez knew he would have to tread very carefully. Toby had a bottomless bank account and to all outward appearances had never done a proper day's work in his life, so his money was coming from somewhere, Jez at first thought he must know that he had a mysterious benefactor keeping him well minted but when he got to know the shallow selfish bastard he realised that he honestly didn't know and didn't care he was scum, a sponger who took from whoever was willing to give and didn't even have the decency to be curious as to who that was. Once when Jez was questioning him he admitted that he thought it must be his birth Mother but also confessed he had never bothered to find her or even ask questions about who she was, he was just happy to accept his good fortune and wasn't interested in her at all. The more Jez got to know Toby or Luke Gerraty as he still called him in the back of his mind the more he disliked him, he found enjoyment in the fact that he knew he would sacrifice this piece of shit to appease his guilt and to cause maximum suffering and pain to

Linda Gerraty his Mother's tormentor, dealer and destroyer, he knew there would be no point inflicting physical pain on her, Linda had always enjoyed physical pain that's why she had made such a good whore and he wanted her to suffer. The night's, the days, the weeks, the months he had spent plotting and planning his revenge. What he would do to her if he ever got the chance but he knew anything he could inflict physically would not be enough to slake his thirst for revenge. Luke had been served up to him on a plate for him to use as he wished to reek that revenge and he intended to use him well and serve him back up to Linda complete with sprigs of Parsley.

Jez knew the time was nearing when he would make himself known to Janelle Ansthruthers. He would descend into her life like a bolt out of the blue and shatter her little smoke screen of respectability and normality. He was going to savour the shock he would cause her most of all, he wanted to see her face, to clock her reaction when she realised her past was coming back to bite her on the arse, he wanted to see the fear in her eye's. He knew what would happen, he knew she would try to keep up the pretence on their initial meet that she would convince herself that he couldn't possibly recognise her, with all her reconstruction work, her new location she would believe that no vestige of her own self existed for him to identify her by. Linda would think she had got away with it, that although their paths had crossed again it was fate a moment in time that would pass, would leave her unchanged, unharmed a chance meeting. But Janelle couldn't be more wrong, Janelle was going to suffer and suffer big time and he was just glad that he was the one that was going to make that happen.

It was time he stepped up a gear and made himself known. He chose a lovely day when the sky was blue and cloudless and by early morning the sun was high burning away the overnight mist, this was done deliberately. Jez had a large tattoo in memory of his Mother just after the attack had happened. He had not only done it through guilt but also as a reminder to Linda every time he was in her bed of what she had done to him and his Mother. It had been his way of flicking the finger and ramming in her face the bond between the man she was quite happy to fuck and the woman she had almost killed it was his own private little retribution and he knew how much it riled her. This morning being so hot already he was wearing a vest shirt knowing that the first thing Linda clocked would be that very tattoo. He had changed over the years, of course he had changed and put on some weight but he was determined to make sure that the woman would have no doubt as to who he really was and that her past had finally caught up with her. He intended to put the fear of God in her from minute one and he knew this blatant display of a symbol from the past would definitely do that. Jez pulled up across the Road from the mock Tudor mansion on the edge of Wentworth golf course, as he had expected her estate was gated and he would need to gain entry via an intercom system, he had already anticipated this when he had heard Pandora and Lou talking about her as a client and how rich and security conscious she was..A far cry from hawking her arse on street corners or working in back street brothels to pay the rent. He approached the gate and pushed the entry button, it was a few seconds before anyone answered but when they did it left him in no doubt as to who lived there even though the tone and modulation had changed slightly through some kind of voice coaching, he still would recognise that voice anywhere. Jez had deliberately made his excuse for calling weak, knowing that once she realised who he was it would unsettle her to know that he was not even bothering to cover his tracks. He said he worked for British Gas and that a gas main had cracked in the street and all homes would lose their supply for two to three hours. Janelle sounded peeved and put out but even more so when he said he would need access to the property to inspect her personal pipe work from the mains as other householders where experiencing problems due to fractured pipe work and shoddy workmanship from when the houses where built. He gave her a number to call if she would prefer to call a superior before he entered her property knowing she would never do it, she was such a smug bitch he knew she would believe she could handle any rapist or madman that tried to assault her. As expected she said this would not be necessary and she buzzed him in. Purposefully Jez adopted his old gait and swagger in case she was watching his approach. If she were watching he was sure something would click into place before he even reached the door and she would already be feeling the hairs on the back of her neck stand to attention. He was never sure if this had worked but when Janelle opened the door her face was a mask of neutrality, her greeting haughty leaving him in no doubt he was dealing with his superior and enforcing his hatred of this cunt.

Janelle stood in front of him but all Jez could see was Linda. His gut instinct on hearing about this woman was spot on. He knew without a shadow of a doubt he was looking at the reincarnation of Linda Gerraty and he also knew that she had realised she was looking into the face of her degraded, debouched past, although he had to give it to her she was good. Not a flicker of recognition passed over her face, nor did she even blink or hesitate but he knew immediately that this was just for show. He knew her heart was racing out of her chest, he knew because he could almost hear it beating could almost taste the tension between them, they were both playing a game of bluff and he knew it. Jez wanted to reach forward and tear this woman's throat out of her neck, he wanted to pick her up and slam her against the wall so hard that he broke every bone in her trunk, fractured every vertebra in her spine, rip her heart from her chest and squeeze it between his fingers. But he couldn't, Jez had enough self control to know that at the end of the day this would not make him feel any better. At the end of the day he would not have achieved the sort of pain and punishment that Linda deserved. He could easily kill her stone dead this minute but he would always regret not making her suffer first, always feel cheated that he had not watched her mental as well as her physical destruction as he had to his Mother's over the years. Jez knew he had to bide his time and the logical part of his brain told him he had waited this long what would a few more weeks matter. So he kept his cool, kept up the pretence that he was an everyday man going about his everyday job but it gave him great pleasure in knowing that Janelle Ansthruthers or Linda Gerraty as he would always think of her until the day he died was frightened. She knew who he was alright and she must have known that this was a sign that she had not seen the last of him. But at the moment Linda was worthy of a BAFTA award. She may very well have got away with her new life her new identity her new name if Jez's hatred hadn't consumed him for so long but unlucky for her it had and BAFTA award or not her acting wouldn't save her now he had found her.

Chapter 22

Janelle was frightened. Janelle was more frightened than she had ever been in her life. She had thought for so many years that she had got away with it, she had covered her tracks and made a new life, on the surface behaved herself for years and yet all of a sudden it felt like her life was crashing down around her ears. Seeing Jez again today a face from the past she thought she would never see again was a huge shock. A shock so close on the heels of Rory's infidelity and consequence disablement she felt like she was stepping back in time, back to her old life, her old ways when every day was aggro, everyday was a struggle to get through unscathed and stay at the top of her tree in the London criminal world. Linda had somehow managed to convince herself she was respectable now, she was a different person, that she was beyond retribution for her past life and crimes. Linda had made everyone believe including herself that she was Janelle Ansthruthers she had reinvented her past and made new friends, spent a large portion of the money she had worked hard to acquire and fitted in with her new surrounding. As far as Janelle was concerned Linda Gerraty wasn't dead, Linda Gerraty had never existed. Paulie was her only link to Linda and by mutual agreement the past was never mentioned when they were together. They had kept their friendship a secret until recently when she needed his help to sort out Rory's betrayal of her but now her friends had become known to him they were still unaware of their past connection. Paulie understood that Linda didn't want reminding of all that happened in the past, that she had successfully blocked it all out of her mind and it suited him fine. He himself had a veneer of respectability about him these days which only disappeared when he was in his old stamping ground, although he seemed to be spending more and more time there recently as money had become a little tight due to his excesses and he needed to return to his old ways to top up funds. But he too wasn't proud of Shirley's downfall, he wasn't proud that in his own mind he should have gone back and finished her off for all of their sake's, but at the time he hadn't had the balls. He always felt a little ashamed that hard man Paulie Santini had copped out. He had been a bastard in those days and didn't baulk at much but going back and looking at Shirley, the mess that Linda had made of her, the flesh hanging off her face, her neck wide open and pumping blood, the stench of burning flesh, he had bottled it and run away. He had grabbed the girl off the balcony, turned his back on Shirley's pleas, the blood gurgling in her lungs as she begged for help, her eye's bulging, her chest heaving and got into his car and driven away. That image and that guilt still haunted him to this day so Janelle's reluctance to talk about it and anything else in their joint unsavoury pasts suited him fine. Janelle knew without ever using words how Paulie felt and she also knew that he felt he had let her down by not going back and killing Shirley, disposing of the body before the Police were involved but she understood that he did not have her incentive. She had done what she had done to Shirley for her Son, her own flesh and blood, the only person she was capable of loving and Paulie didn't understand that, he just didn't have the same instinct to protect, that unconditional all consuming love that had pushed Linda to the most violent, the most sickening, the most devastating act of her whole life.

Janelle's mind was bought back to the present, she wasn't stupid enough to believe that Jez had landed on her doorstep by mistake and she definitely wasn't stupid enough to believe he worked for British Gas and he knew that. She had known of his whereabouts on the club scene for years. Although she no longer employed Danny her old minder for Luke because when she left she did not keep in touch, the less people that knew where she was the better but she had continued to use other agencies to keep tabs on her Son, her past and old enemies and friends. Linda wanted to keep an eye on Luke for obvious reasons but Jez because she always knew he would come looking for her, she was well aware they had unfinished business and knew she had to watch her back. She could kick herself now, she had become complacent over the last few years, she had got lazy and indolent, let herself become too comfortable. That was why all this shit with Rory had happened, she had let things slide, taken her eye off the ball and now it had all come back to smack her in the face. Linda was frightened alright she was shitting herself and for the third time in her life she knew that there was only one person that could help her and that was Paulie Santini.

Janelle was just about to make the call when self doubt kicked in. What if she had misjudged Paulie? What if it had been Paulie who had led Jez to her whereabouts and new identity? What if Paulie had decided as he got older that he could live with his own guilt anymore and to sort his own conscience out he had sold her down the river? Janelle didn't like all these poisonous thoughts that were bombarding her brain, assaulting her senses but she knew she had no choice but to face them. She had to ask the questions, come up with the answers that filled the gaps in the puzzle before she made the call and put all her trust in Paulie again. Janelle would never have doubted Paulie's loyalty on any other matter but she had suspected for all these years that his guilt had been growing like a cancer growing inside him, choking him, ageing him before his time and had caused the only true rift between them for all their years of friendship. Linda needed to sit down and analyse her feelings properly for Paulie, since he had come back into her life to sort out the problem of Rory her old feelings of affection for him had returned and he was already providing the sex that Rory could no longer manage to give her, but she frightened these feelings might be clouding her judgement and Paulie could be running for both camps. Janelle was getting old. She didn't need all this shit falling on her head at the moment she had learned to enjoy the quiet life even though she still made her money from the clubs she hadn't been near them for years. They were all run by faceless accountants, brokers and managers now all she did was provide the bank account details for the money to keep pouring into, she had no real interest or knowledge of what went on in them these days nor did she have any desire to. Life moved on and she thought life had moved on very nicely for her until the last few weeks, on reflection she knew that Paulie would never betray her and that he would be as surprised as she had been to see Jez resurface in her life after all these years. Linda was desperately trying to believe that Jez hadn't recognised her but her heart was telling her different, she wanted to turn around and run away again but she knew she couldn't, she knew she had to face the music that time in her new charmed life had run out and she knew she needed that help. Linda knew she had to get help fast, she knew that now Jez had found her he would exact his revenge, she had always known it. Even when Jez had returned to her bed a few days after she had maimed his Mother she knew it was for a purpose, she knew he would do for her one day and that knowledge had played a large part in her disappearance in the first place. That knowledge had kept her awake at night and that knowledge had burnt constantly at the back of her brain since the day she left the East End of London almost twenty years ago.

Linda called Paulie. When she thought of it afterwards she couldn't believe how calm she was, she couldn't believe that she managed to hold a normal conversation without relaying the panic and fear in her voice. She knew she had to find out more about what Paulie was up to these days, his acquaintance his circle of friends, she realised she had been a fool in the last few months not to find out about this part of his life.

The occasional meeting and phone calls they had exchanged over the years, hadn't included any discussions about their business dealings friendship and sex had been more important, their business lives no longer crossed and it had made their relationship better. The old attractions had always been there and they liked to feed off each others perversions and this had been the basis of their new relationship since Paulie had been back in her life as an almost permanent fixture. But now she had to do some digging.

"Paulie how are you doing? Busy?"

"You know how it is, some days are busier than others, some I don't stop others I'm sitting here pulling my dick thinking of you darling" he laughed

"Don't be sick!" she snapped' the acid in her voice alerted Paulie to the fact something was seriously wrong she had always enjoyed him talking dirty to her, always enjoyed it when he gave her the graphic details of his fantasies over the phone but today she was not playing.

"What's up sweetheart, unlike you not to want to know what I'm thinking about doing to you later?"

"Paulie I'm sorry, just tired I suppose, having Rory home is just getting me down, all that equipment all over the place and that fucking nurse always sticking her nose in."

"Then get rid of them both, you don't even like the cunt anymore I don't know what your trying to do, is it to make yourself look good to the Doctors or because your frightened there'll be some come back on you? You know that isn't going to happen, I made sure there was no connection to you, you know I did."

"I know that but I just like seeing the cunt suffer. I like to look at his face knowing that his brains still working perfectly that he knows that he has me to thank for his life as it is, that I could have had him dispatched to St Peter if I'd wanted to..I like him to know that he is here due to my mercy and when that hard nosed cunt goes home of a day he is left to my tender ministrations. It's the smell, the noise the sanctimonious old cunt that treats him like her baby and me like a piece of shit I have just had enough it's getting me down that's all"

"You sure?"

"Yes Paulie I am fucking sure."

"O.k. I'm not busy today shall I come over and make you feel better darling see what uncle Paulie's got in his pocket to make you feel better?"

"Paulie I told you I'm not in the mood just leave it out O.K. come over for dinner but don't go expecting anything else got it? I could do with a friend tonight though"

"Right I'll be over by seven, do I bring anything other than my gorgeous self?"

Linda wanted to tell him to bring his gun, his baseball bat, his knuckle dusters, cyanide, arsenic or anything else he could get his fucking hands on but she knew she couldn't she knew she had to keep calm and see what he had to say first. Once she saw Paulie face to face she knew she would be able to tell if he was lying, if for the first time in their long friendship he had let her down and would be useless to her in this latest pile of shit. She was silently praying that this wasn't the case because she needed Paulie now more than she had ever needed him in her whole life.

Chapter 23

Paulie tied up all his loose ends and made his way over to Janelle's. He loved it there, he loved all the opulence of the tree lined streets, every house being detached, huge remote controlled gates that everyone found an absolute necessity and the stunning views across Wentworth golf course with its flawless greens and swanky nineteenth hole golf club. As you got closer and closer to his old friends home you could almost smell and taste the money in the air, you had to be seriously well heeled to live here and over the years Janelle had amassed enough money to fit in nicely. Not that Paulie would want to live here permanently, he liked London he liked noise, dirt and hustle and bustle he wasn't cut out for country living. Paulie was still a regular face on the London club scene although an ageing one but that had never stopped him getting the fanny and occasional recreational drugs that he craved. Paulie was still a womaniser, still liked them young, still liked to initiate them into his perversions and he still managed to pull the best looking birds around. He knew in his heart this probably had more to do with his money and rep as he had never kidded himself that he was a beauty let alone now when he was greying, the paunch was growing and his face was beginning to look like a map of spaghetti junction but he had a presence and a twinkle in his eye which made sure he did alright with the women. Paulie now owned a bachelor pad at Chelsea Harbour which was hardly ever without a female guest, money in the bank, friends and he enjoyed the lifestyle that he led. He had never felt that he needed to settle down, never craved a family although on several occasions he had got the blame for knocking a girl up and walking away but he never saw that as his problem, it was theirs, if they couldn't look after themselves what did he care. Paulie had no intention of being tied down by some little tart with an eye on his wallet. He was happy as he was and bollocks to anyone who didn't like it.

Paulie had been pleased when Janelle had seemed to want him a s a regular visitor in his life after he had helped her out with that piece of shit she called a Husband. He had always thought of her over the years and when they met up they always ended up in bed but now their relationship was becoming more intimate again not just sex but friendship too and although he didn't like to admit he was getting to an age where friendship was becoming more and more important. He liked the fact that he could talk to Janelle and not just fuck her, he liked the fact that they enjoyed the same things and that they could even go out for the day without him being embarrassed by her like he often was with his little bimbos. Every man has to accept at some time in their lives that they need more than just a leg over, it's a shock but it's life and finally those feelings where creeping into to Paulie's subconscious. When he was at Janelle's these days he had started to feel comfortable and at peace but he still loved his London life.

Paulie reached Janelle's and didn't bother to buzz in, he had been given his own remote to the impressive black and gold gates when they had got back together and he didn't feel he needed to announce his arrival every time he paid a visit. He parked his car next to her Merc in the garage and entered the house through the side door. The only thing he didn't like about this place was that it was always quiet. Paulie liked a bit of noise, the first thing he would do when he walked through his own front door was hit the play button on his state of the art stereo, blast out the neighbours with Bruce Springstein, Bon Jovi and Dire Straights, all singers that showed his age but he didn't care he liked them, he just couldn't get into all this R&B and garage which was all they seemed to play at the clubs these days, he liked his rock. He called out to Janelle so as not to startle her when he walked into the Kitchen which was where he knew she would be. Since moving here Janelle had become a brilliant cook, from not being able to boil an egg she could now put Gordon Ramsey to shame she loved to spend all her time in the Kitchen and had honed her skills to Gourmet standard in a very short time. The Kitchen was her hub, very much her pride and joy and what a Kitchen it was. Janelle had one wall made into huge sliding doors that allowed light to stream in and when open in the summer gave the room a feel of infinity. The room was absolutely massive and everything in it had been picked for its practicality and design by Janelle herself. Everywhere you looked there were work tops to prepare and display food and drink, one whole wall a wine rack complete with chillier and humidifier depending if it displayed red or white and the main feature was an island accommodating the biggest range Paulie had ever seen in a domestic Kitchen. Janelle had needed to get it commissioned as the only comparable one's being industrial and didn't have the look she required for her inner sanctum.

    When he entered the room Janelle was busy peeling and chopping the vegetables for tonight's meal, she stood staring out of the window whilst leaning over the triple sink and seemed ignorant to his presence. He walked over and put his arm around her shoulder and moved in for a friendly peck on the cheek but she jumped back in amazement and narrowly missed slicing his ear of with the precision sharp knife she was using to prepare the food.

    "You silly fucker what is wrong with you creeping up on me like that" she spat at him as she tried to regain her composure.

    "Babe I didn't fucking creep up on you I've been screaming at you all the way down the fucking hall you stupid bitch you could have killed me with that fucking thing, what is wrong with you today?"

    "Nothing, nothing you just made me jump that's all, old habits die hard, thought I was back on the streets then, it's been a while since I had to use that manoeuvre, sorry, O.K I am sorry just get us both a drink and then we can calm down a bit"

"Janelle what the fuck is wrong, please just tell me, you never want to talk about the past so why now and why are you so bloody jumpy I am sick of this Janelle just let's get it off your chest ah, has something happened, something gone wrong?"

"Just maudlin that's all, the past sometimes comes back and bites you on the arse doesn't it, don't you ever feel that?"

"Don't I just" Paulie was thinking about a bit of agg he'd had at a club a few weeks ago and only yesterday he'd had a visit from the Old Bill trying to find out his part in the proceedings, but Janelle jumped down his throat.

"What do you mean? What problems have you got from the past? What are you not telling me Paulie are you hiding something because if you are I should know what's going on, if you don't tell me your not playing fair, all this shit about the past I thought we left it all behind years ago"

"What are you talking about Janelle? I think you better start telling me what's going on and now, stop pulling my chain and give me the facts. You are like a cat on a hot tin roof, all over the place and giving me all this shit about being tired and that cunt Rory upstairs just tell me what is happening. You're the fucking one who doesn't want to revisit the past and talk about old times not me so stop treating me like a fool and just tell me what has frightened you"

"Jez"

"Jez, Jez Watson what about him, none of us has seen that little fucker for years what have you got to worry about him for?"

"He's been here Paulie, he came here today and I am one hundred fucking percent sure that he knows who I am"

"Just calm down and tell me what happened, are you sure it was Jez, are you sure you haven't got it wrong, you wouldn't even know what he looked like now maybe your just stretching yourself too much at the moment."

"Paulie don't treat me like a fucking idiot I assure you it was Jez."

"How do you know, tell me Janelle how the fuck can you be sure it was Jez Watson did he introduce himself, did he walk up to you and say remember me Linda?"

"Don't be fucking patronising, I would know him anywhere of course I would for God's sake I've known him since he was born and he hasn't changed that much since I saw him last but it was that tattoo, you remember that tattoo that he had done just after it all kicked off, that great big fucking thing that covered most of his right arm. Something in Latin about honour in death"

"That's common, something to do with the Para's or the fucking army you know that little fucker fancied himself as a hard man, loads of blokes have got that"

"No Paulie this was different, he designed this himself, used to flaunt it whenever he could, used to tell people it was in honour of his sick Mother. I am not likely to forget the fucking thing it used to well rile me and he knew it."

"But why would he come here now? Why today? What did he say did he threaten you or lay a finger on you if he did I'll have that little cunts bollocks on a plate."

"He didn't say anything about the past, just pretend he had come to check a gas main but he hardly tried to disguise himself did he? He was putting the frighteners on, rubbing my fucking nose in it he knows who I am I swear it"

"How can he Jan you look nothing like you used to, don't sound the same and no-one but me knows where you are. As far as I know he doesn't have anything to do with the clubs anymore and he was never into the drugs so how would he track you down?"

"I don't care, he knows who I am and I know it, I was beginning to think you had sold me down the river, I would be wrong wouldn't I Paulie?"

"Fucking hell Janelle I could fucking stripe you, why would I of all fucking people tell him where you are I haven't even seen him for years, I never did like the fucking tosser we were hardly likely to stay best buddies were we? You have some fucking nerve woman, what do you think I am?"

"Sorry Paulie I am truly sorry, he just rattled me I know he recognised me, someone must have found out about me and tipped him off. It's been so long, we've kept this thing tight so why the fuck does this have to happen now?"

"I don't know Janelle but I can assure you it is fuck all to do with me. What does he want?"

"He didn't ask for anything he just wanted me to know who he was not why he was here."

"O.K, we'll do some asking around, see what he's been up to lately, see who he's been seeing lately just don't let it get to you we'll sort it what can he do anyway, this place is like Fort Knox and I'll move in for a while, there's no worries we'll find out what he wants."

"Paulie I thought I was finished with all this, I don't want to go back to all that do you think he wants money? If that's what he wants then he can have it, I'll give it to him I just want him out of my life, I don't want to have anything more to do with him now'

'Janelle it will get sorted. We are all too old for this shit Jez included. I will find him, find out how he found you and find out what he wants I promise you"

"Thank you Paulie I just can't have this thing hanging over my head much longer it will fucking do me in!"

"It's not a problem Janelle just give me some time"

Paulie was worried; although he would never let Janelle see it he was shitting himself. What did that bastard want and why now? If Paulie were honest he had always known that Jez would come after Janelle one day, that he could never swallow his Mother's treatment walk away and forget it. Paulie also knew through the grapevine that Shirley had just died but he wouldn't tell Janelle that. Paulie had known the Hospital that Shirley had been in for years and the Hospice she was then moved to when time was running out, he had even visited her a few times, after all at one time they had been more than just good friends and he did feel guilty about not putting her out of her misery. Was that why Jez had turned up now, had his own feelings of guilt finally overwhelmed him when she met her delayed end, that was a possibility because no way did Paulie believe that fate had bought him to Janelle's door however much he tried to convince her that was the case. Had Jez always known where she was and just been waiting for the opportunity to make his move? Paulie could not guess but he was now charged with the job of finding out. He would protect Janelle anyway that he could, she was the only woman he had ever come close to loving and it was his job to make sure Jez never got close to her again.

Chapter 24

Jez went away from Janelle's with an odd feeling of defeat. He knew now what he had to do, the conclusion to all his years of pain. He just had to work out how he wanted to do it. He wanted Janelle to suffer; he wanted her to suffer the pain and degradation his Mother had suffered for all those years. The problem was that deep down Jez didn't really have the heart for it all, although in his youth he had been a spiteful vicious little bastard it had always been for gain not pleasure. He had needed to behave that way to survive. All the violence, the spite, the pain and hurt he had inflicted on other people had all been for him and his Mother to carry on existing, to put food on the table and keep his Mother in drugs and happy. Keep his Mother off the streets and accepting anything any Man wanted to do to her to keep herself going. But over the years Jez had lost his edge, he didn't need money, he didn't need friends and he definitely didn't need to go backwards and get involved again with his dark past but he had to, something kept pulling him back making him bitter and twisted about his Mothers life and her treatment at Linda's hands. It all kept rearing it's ugly head and bringing back all the guilt he had felt that day when he left her close to death on the filthy floor of that flat in Peckham, alone, beaten her skin frying in acid but her eye's still pleading with him. Those same eye's that had pleaded with him to go out and steal for her when he was a child and she was writhing around the floor in agony because she needed her next fix and wasn't capable to go and fuck a punter for it. The same eye's that had watched him from that shrunken, hairless skull every time he visited her in Hospital since the attack, the haunting all knowing eye's that although she couldn't communicate with words she could use her eye's to reprimand him. Everyone thought she was mad, beyond reason or communication but every time Jez looked into those eyes's he was reliving that day in that flat along with her. Her eyes knew what he had done and he now understood that the eyes were the window to the soul. Jez could see straight into his Mother's troubled mind and soul and the pain that lay there and he always felt he had caused that pain by letting her down. The abandonment that he saw in those eyes was what scorched his heart picked at his brain and gave him nightmares every night. That abandonment would stay with him until the day of his own death, he had to avenge his Mother, he had to stay strong and carry out what he was sure would have been his Mother's wishes and he would make sure he did it in his Mothers name. if he got caught, if he went down none of it mattered he would carry out his duty whilst he still walked this Earth and accept the consequences both now and in the here after and then he could, at last rest in peace.

Jez knew the best way to hurt Linda was to get to her through her Son as his own Mother Shirley had known all those years ago when she tried to cross Linda. Linda cared only about her Son always had and always would and as luck would have it, he had just fallen into Jez's hands. He had known from the first moment he had set eyes on Toby who he was, had pulled up the memories from that locked dark space in his mind that he had seen this Man before, but not as a Man as a swaggering drugged up teenager lying in a filthy bed, in a filthy flat with a drug addicted whore twice his age laying beside him. He had saved him the embarrassment of his Mother finding him in that situation and the whore's skin from being ripped from her body piece by piece by Linda. If Linda had found her precious Son with such a piece of shit she would have been dead and buried. Linda had a short memory, she had been as bad if not worse than that woman, so had his own Mother, they had all been ruined by drugs, dragged up in poverty and done what they had to do to survive, but not her Luke, Linda thought that he was better than anyone else, he was special, he was pure, she had managed to block out from her reasoning that Luke was the same as Jez. They had both been dragged out of a whore's body, no idea of who or where their Fathers were or how many other men had used their Mothers bodies while they were nestling in their wombs, no thought for any disease they could or might have been born with no hope for their emotional and mental development because of their Mothers lifestyles before they were even born. Linda had sanctified Luke and in doing so had sanctified herself. She had seen herself as a hard woman, an achiever a success but she had conveniently forgotten that she had been as dirtier bitch as the rest of them if not worse, had firstly sucked, fucked and done anything else necessary to get on her way, then trodden on the backs of other unfortunate women like his Mother to claw her way up to her elevated status as a Madame and a dealer and now all these years later to a respectable housewife with a lovely home, plenty of money but a poor disabled Husband to care for which got her respect and compassion from the neighbours. What a fucking joke, if that Man had came to an unfortunate accident then Jez was sure Linda would have made that accident happen. People around her, in her inner circle, her coven only ever got hurt when she wanted them to be hurt otherwise they were cosseted, protected and looked after, if Rory Ansthruthers had the rest of his life to look forward to in a wheelchair he had his Wife to thank for it.

Jez had honestly began to believe that the heart to sort out this mess wasn't in him anymore but the more he thought about all these misdemeanours the more he ruminated on the past and his anger at Linda's easy comfortable life, the more he realised he actually hadn't changed, not really he realised he would always have the same heart, the black heart he had been born with and used until he became old enough to realise his bad ways and want to change them but like he had said often enough about Linda Gerraty, a leopard doesn't change it's spots, it just uses them as camouflage. His heart was as black as the day he was born into a world he had had to drag himself up in, a world that had given him nothing and this woman and her spoiled brat everything his heart desired. He had no compassion no sympathy no kindred bond with this Man who was another Whore's Son so he knew that he didn't really have to call upon all his debased, violent ruthless hidden feelings to carry out his job, they had never really gone away they had just been laying dormant under the surface waiting for the opportunity for a chink in the armour of his nice safe dependable façade and that chink had just become a fucking great hole. The only difference with the new Jez to the old one was that he no longer jumped at his prey like a hungry tiger, he was older had more patience he had time to sit back and think about what he wanted to do and the most effective way to do it. He didn't want mistakes and when he had executed his plan he wanted to sit back and watch Linda suffer, he wanted to watch her pain watch her fall apart in front of his very eyes and he wanted to enjoy every minute it of it. Jez was going to enjoy watching Linda learn that it was him that had taken her precious Sons life but he wanted to do it in his own time. Firstly he would witness the absolute destruction of that cunt that he had once thought of as a lover and a friend he would watch her suffer, watch her die a little day by day until her grief was so deep she felt she couldn't take anymore and when he had made her reach that point when he was watching her withering and dying with the only pain she could not bare couldn't handle and could do nothing to stop he would finally go in for the kill, show his hand and make sure she knew that he was responsible for it all. That she knew it was Jez that had bought her to this that she had finally lost, Linda Gerraty had finally got her just deserts from the Son of her old Friend Shirley the boy that she had helped make the Man that he was now, the boy that she had taken as her lover before he was barely old enough to know what his own dick was for let alone let her use it and abuse him like she did. But she was about to learn that the Man that they had both shaped knew what every bit of his body was for now and that was to ensure the downfall of the house of Gerraty. Every muscle bone and sinew in Jez's body had been highly tuned and trained for all these years to do this job and now the time was near that they would all be called into action to do their job, if he withered up and died after this task, so be it he didn't care one bit he would die fulfilled. Perhaps that was why he had never settled down, never had kids never wanted to let people get too close because ultimately he knew at the end of the day his life would be over when he had taken his revenge his days on Earth would be numbered one way or another and he wouldn't inflict that on anyone else. He would not leave a child on this Earth without a Father, he would not leave anyone else with his responsibilities and he didn't want to think of a child inheriting the kinks of his personality, his determination and his hatred. For years Jez had thought that it was just that he didn't trust women all the women in his young life had been liars cheats and whores so as he grew older he kept his distance but with this new awareness of his self and his motivations he realised that his feelings had gone much deeper, his true feelings had been buried and hidden even from himself until that woman appeared back in his life again. now like an atom bomb those feelings were mushrooming out from their inner core and poisoning everything they came into contact with polluting his system infecting his being body and soul and churning up what lay beneath the respectable calm sensible image he had built up over the years. The old Jez was back and back for good and Linda would find that out when he was ready to make it known and not before.

    Jez knew he was forced to continue his relationship with Lou and Toby until he had made his final plans, he knew he had to play the smiling amigo although he felt nothing but contempt for Toby. He could not find it in his heart to feel any sort of pity for the Man that had come from Linda Gerraty his hatred was so deep. He set about perfecting his façade that everything was O.K and that he was enjoying their company at the same time as making his future arrangements, he didn't intend to give Linda any chance to protect her Son or save him from his fate as she had before he wanted to make it clean and clinical with no room for mistakes he wanted the shock alone to be enough to kill her. Jez knew that Linda would now be more vigilante after he had made his appearance at her home, he had made sure she had recognised him and he knew she would be on edge expecting something to happen which had been his intention, to rattle her cage. He also knew he would be getting a visit from the ever faithful Paulie Santini. Linda had spent years fucking that bloke around pulling his strings dangling him on a chain and thinking she was in charge but in an unguarded moment years ago Paulie had admitted that although he loved the bones of the woman he didn't really want her. Paulie was of the old school, you fuck women like Linda because they'll do anything to please you, let you do anything to them but their not the sort of women you take home to Mum and when you sit and think about it they are also letting any other bloke do the same and with a whore rather than a little tart it's even worse. How many times has she done this before? How many men have been there today? What has she had or worse still what has she got?' What wouldn't she do for money?' Paulie had admitted to Jez all these thoughts were at the back of his mind every time he fucked and he knew although he had huge affection for her and a strange kind of love he could never enjoy sex with her to marry her. She looked good, had changed to the consummate professional madam at that time but Paulie always said he couldn't forget that she used to give blow jobs for a fiver a time and was never fussy about whose dick she sucked and he could never fully put that out of his mind.

Jez knew that when Paulie came calling it would be as a friend not as an enemy because even though they had never really liked each other especially when Jez had become Linda's plaything but they had found a unity on that fateful day as they watched his Mother literally drowning in her own blood her flesh disintegrating her breath gasping, as they stood together against the police gaining any evidence that might implicate Linda in the crime and as they pulled together to ensure Luke's safe return to his Parents. They had exposed their fear and feelings to each other that day, maybe unintentionally but due to the business they had been involved in they had to ensure each others loyalty and trust to stay free and achieve their aims. Jez was certain Paulie would remember all this and that it would hold him in good stead when Paulie made his visit. But what Jez also knew about himself was that he had the steely resolve, the burning hatred and the maturity to be able to hide his true feelings from Paulie Santini. Paulie would be there to find out his intentions. He would know that Jez's meeting with Janelle Ansthruthers was in no way an accident that it had been a deliberate call and he would want to know why but what his visit to Jez would confirm to him was that Linda was running scared, it had been his intention all along to shit her up and he knew she would go straight to Paulie and Paulie's visit would be confirmation of his success so he was looking forward to seeing him.

Chapter 25

Paulie arrived at Jez's as expected still good looking, still confidant and still outwardly the cool calm businessman. He walked into Jez's office at the agency as if he was a frequent visitor walking straight up to Jez and pushing his hand out to greet him with a big wide smile on his handsome clock.

"Jez, mate, long time no see"

"Paulie, how you doing what brings you to this neck of the woods, not your territory is it, is this business or pleasure?"

"Pleasure Son, pleasure just doing a bit locally and thought I'd drop in"

"Paulie you don't work locally and you've never just dropped in before in all the years I've lived around here so cut to the chase and tell me what the problem is!"

"O.K Jez you know what the problem is, our mutual friends not happy Jez she wants to know what her visit was about, bit amateurish for you wasn't it I thought you had more imagination to be honest mate"

"Just checking things out Paulie I heard a rumour she was in the area so I thought I'd revisit the good old day's know what I mean" he said with a wink

"Then why didn't you say hello instead of pulling that fucking gas Man shit?"

"You mean she didn't find it funny then?"

"Fuck off Jez you knew she wouldn't. Linda's Janelle now, new life, new Woman the past is the past mate we've all changed"

"Have we Paulie, have we really? How did Linda's Husband land up in a wheelchair then? Tragic accident? Did the poor shit have an illness or did he meet someone in a dark alley one night because he pissed his Wife off? Tell me Paulie have you ever wondered what happened? Oh no sorry I forgot you wouldn't have wondered would you, you wouldn't have had to wonder would you because you were there. You were the hard Man that sorted him for her because he went over the side weren't you. You were the one that condemned him to that fucking wheelchair and a life of misery with that wicked old cunt."

"Where are you hearing all this from Jez? Why are you listening to fairy tales at your time of life?"

"No fairy tale Paulie, fact. I've done my homework see don't worry mate I know exactly what's been going on."

"Jez what is all this cock and bull about? Why after all this time I thought you'd got out of all this I thought it was all over years ago"

"No Paulie you thought that she had won and in a way she did. She took my Mother away and made me play a part in her downfall. I was a kid Paulie a fucking kid and I had to watch my Mother die like that because believe me she might have been existing for the last fucking twenty years but she died on the carpet in that flat in front of my eyes as far as I'm concerned."

"Jez don't make me fucking laugh what sort of a Mother was she to you, she was never there, treated you like shit, you weren't brought up you were fucking dragged up what did she ever do for you for you to suddenly have so much loyalty. When you were sticking it to Linda were you ever thinking of what that did to your fucking Mother, were you ever worried about her fucking feelings then?"

"Piss off Paulie that's not the fucking same and you know it"

"Jez you've got selective memory mate anyway where do you go from here? What happens now? You need to know I will still stand her corner nothings changed there!"

"What sort of wanker are you Paulie, after all this time what is it with you don't even fucking want her full time couldn't bring yourself to fuck her without thinking of where she's been, what's your problem now, getting old? Getting soft? Perhaps old whores are all you can pull these days ah?"

"Don't try and rile me Jez, I aint taking this shit from you all I'm here to say is if your gonna restart the war then I am behind her all the way"

"No problem mate, no problem you've said your piece now do you want a drink for old times sake or are you going back to have your belly rubbed for being a good boy?"

"I'll drink with you Jez, I don't bare any grudges to you, you know that Jez let's just drop the subject and have a shant for the good times'

"O.K scotch is it or has that changed "

"Scotch is great, that's never changed mate Scotch has always been my weakness"

They spent the next few hours in relatively comfortable conversation about the past and the intervening years which had led their lives along very different paths. Jez along the almost straight and narrow, Paulie still with his fingers stuck in every pie his drugs and clubs still playing a big part in his fortune amassing, women coming and going, not really seeing Linda at all that much but keeping in touch at a distance mostly. This was the part that interested Jez, this was were he was trying to navigate the conversation to and he was starting to achieve his goal. Jez had never been much of a drinker but Paulie had obviously forgotten that over the years. Whilst Paulie was downing scotch like there was no tomorrow Jez had been drinking American dry, Paulie had failed to notice that Jez was not adding any alcohol to it, over the years the alcohol had taken effect on him his dulled his edge made him reticent. He talked too much and didn't think before he said what popped into his head. He used to be able to hold his drink but Jez knew as soon as he had entered the office that he was into the scotch big time these days., it wasn't only the stale smell of drink it was also the ruddy complexion, the slight yellow tinge to the white's of his eyes that all gave the game away and Jez had decided in a split second that he would use this weakness to his advantage. And so far it was working, working like a fucking dream.

Jez had already found out the horrific details of Rory Anstruthers attack at the hands of Paulie and the instructions of Linda he had also Managed to find out that she know had very little contact with her Son which broke her heart but he was an adult and had chosen to have no real contact with his birth Mother but she still had an update now and again from another source, still trying to keep the chord attached to a Son that had no interest in her whatsoever. Jez definitely knew that his association with Toby had not yet come to Linda's attention, that she was unaware of the circles he had been moving in for the last few months or that he had a huge cocaine habit that someone probably her was financing behind the scenes. Paulie kept trying to encourage Jez to call Linda Janelle but he wouldn't bend on that one. Linda would always be Linda to him, he had to keep the memory of the old Linda alive in his mind to keep the venom dripping through his veins. He had to think of Linda Gerraty as tart, gangster, madam to think of her as Janelle Ansthruthers, housewife, devoted carer and middle class doyen wouldn't work for him it would knock the rough edges off his resolve and make him weak, so Linda it would always be to Jez Watson. Paulie wasn't happy with this but fuck Paulie what did he matter anyway he was pissing Jez off now the more he drank the more maudlin he became for what he kept calling the good old days, what fucking good old days, Jez couldn't remember any of them being too good for him. He needed to get rid of him soon, he'd had enough, he just wanted him to fuck off back to where he'd come from now, he didn't need him anymore, he wanted his own space to start planning and organising the job in hand, plan his next move. In the end he made an excuse, told Paulie he had another appointment that he couldn't put off, said he was sorry but that he had to kick him out and get on with the business of the day. Paulie took it well, in his drunken state he didn't realise he was getting the 'brush off', he got up to leave and nearly fell arse over head. Jez called him a cab but was not happy, this meant the cunt would have to return to collect his car and to be honest Jez had seen enough of him to last a lifetime. He cancelled the cab, decided to take Paulie and his car back to Linda and give her a nice little surprise. He knew full well she wouldn't be happy when he turned up, Paulie in tow pissed as a rat but that just added to the fun of it.

Jez steadied Paulie in the lift on the way to the basement car park and shoved him into the passenger seat none too gently. Paulie was out like a light the minute his head hit the head rest, Jez pulled out of the car park and turned right into the stream of traffic that would take him South to Linda's house on the edge of Wentworth golf course the journey would take a good hour so he knew that Paulie would be well and truly out for the count and sleeping like a buffalo by the time they arrived which suited him fine, he relaxed back into the luxury of the cream leather upholstery and felt it mould around his body. Paulie had always been a flash bastard and this car was no exception a midnight blue top of the range Jaguar XJR with all the extras, Paulie liked throwing his money around and this car was no exception. Jez switched on the CD and Norah Jones smooth and mellow blasted out, he was going to enjoy this journey as long as he could, switch off from the low groaning snores that Paulie was emitting from the passenger seat beside him and enjoy the ride. For the first time he realised just how old Paulie had become and he felt quite sorry for the old fucker. He must be knocking sixty and he was still trying to play the field running around after Linda like a love sick puppy at the same time as pretending to be the best lay in town, what did he think he was. Looking at him now Jez could see in truth he was just a pathetic, desperate and lonely old Man craving his youth and a woman like Linda's attention again God for bid that the rest of us should end up like that sad lonely and living in the past which wasn't so good when it was the present in fact it was fucking awful and to crave all that again was a fucking tragedy on a grand scale.

When he reached Linda's he buzzed the intercom and her viewing screen showed Paulie's car waiting to enter she didn't wonder why he had not used his remote and didn't hesitate to open the gates and let him in. Jez wished he had brought a camera when she opened the front door and saw him standing there the look of horror on her face and the pure fear that flitted across it was a memory he would cherish but he wished he had been able to capture it on film. She didn't fuck around this time pretending she didn't know him though she came straight to the point.

"What the fuck are you doing here again Jez?"

"Nice way to speak to an old friend who's come to bring a special delivery for you!"

"What, what are you talking about?"

"Paulie, he's in the car pissed out of his head, of course I can't say brain because I'm not sure he's got one these days but definitely out of his head."

"So where did you find him and why bring him to my door?"

"Don't fuck around Linda," he used her old name deliberately to get a rise out of her

"You know he has been with me because you sent him give me some fucking credit will you?"

"Will you stop swearing on my doorstep and bring him in"

"Frightened of what the neighbours might think? What people thought of you Linda never used to make you lose any sleep?"

"Jez please, just shut up and bring him in" she turned on her heels and marched back into the house only glancing over her shoulder once to see Jez throw Paulie over his own shoulder making sure he had blasted the horn as he pulled Paulie over the seats and whistling at the top of his voice for good measure just in case any of her neighbours were beaking.

Linda was seriously rattled. What was this cunt doing turning up on her doorstep causing as much agg as possible and bringing Paulie back pissed out of his box to boot, what was going on here. Jez walked confidently into the house pushed Paulie onto a sofa in the lounge where he began to grunt and groan like a stuck pig and marched on further into the kitchen where he'd seen Linda disappear to.

"Servants quarters for your old friend then is it Linda?"

"The name is Janelle Jez, Janelle Ansthruthers and don't forget it. Now what's the game? Why have you suddenly resurfaced and why are you haunting me?"

Jez was staring past Linda to the conservatory where a good looking bloke in his thirties was sitting in a wheelchair staring out into the garden his body broken and useless. A nurse dressed from head to foot in white sat close to him reading from a book and giving him a drink when he needed one from a baby's beaker through a straw. The Man was big; at present his frame still intact the muscle wasting hadn't yet set in. Jez knew from watching his Mother's deterioration that those muscles would shrivel and die through lack of use and however hard you tried you could never get the tone and strength back that this Man would be trapped a little more day by day and be left at the mercy of those around him for all his physical needs. Jez ignored Linda and walked into the conservatory greeting the nurse with a cheery

"Afternoon, turning into another nice one" he was shocked when not only did the nurse answer but so did Rory, a broken husky voice confirmed the weather conditions and then fell back into total silence. Jez realised the poor fucker still had all his faculties, his body was the only problem and that bitch had caused his disability, this poor sod was worse off than even his Mother had been, at least Shirley hadn't known what day it was didn't have a clue as to what was going on around her and in a way she was happy in her own world that she had created over the years, but this bloke didn't even have oblivion to escape to. Jez would lay money on that being Linda's intention, she would tease torment and ridicule him because he had dared to betray made her look a fool. For all her changes all her outward respectability the cunt hadn't changed just as he knew she wouldn't have, her heart was still pumping poison, her soul sold to the devil when she was only a child, he began to feel all the bile and bitterness rise in his throat but he kept steady and walked back into the kitchen where Linda was standing with a large scotch in her hand.

"Don't I get one of those after all these years and returning your boyfriend to you safe and sound and I don't even get offered a snifter"

"What do you want" she said trying to hold back the annoyance in her voice

"Mineral water thanks, helps me keep a clear head"

Linda crossed the room to the imposing fridge and took out a bottle of Windsor House. Jez had to laugh at this Windsor House; there was a time when this woMan couldn't even afford tap water let alone this trendy bottled stuff. Linda noted the smile cross his face and wouldn't give him the satisfaction of asking what he had found funny, she passed him his drink and he sat down at the counter.

"Drink your drink and go please Jez I don't want any trouble, this is my life now and I don't want to revisit the past."

"We were old lovers Linda not just old friends don't' you ever think about the things we used to do together or should I say the things you got me to do. Don't you ever miss all our old friends and want to catch up with what their doing with their lives?" His voice dripped with sarcasm.

"No Jez I told you I am not Linda anymore how Many times do I have to tell you I am Janelle the past is the past and I want none of it"

"I just thought I'd let you know about your old friend Shirley mate, remember her, my Mother, well she died a few months ago, not a nice death but there again not a nice life so a happy release wouldn't you agree? I thought you couldn't have heard because I didn't see you at the funeral, not you, not Paulie not any of the old crowd"

"Are you mad? Why would I want to go to the funeral after what she did to me why would I want to say goodbye to that no good piece of shit?"

Jez sprang across the room and held her jaw in his clasp having already closed the door on the conservatory he knew he could not be seen by either Rory or the nurse not that he cared if he could.

"Now Linda, that is not nice, you were friends once, worked together not even averse to doing a double if a punter could pay for it so didn't you owe her something?"

"After what she did to Luke I owed her nothing and I still don't I was glad to hear that she'd finally gone, glad that she suffered the way she did"

Jez squeezed her cheeks tighter as he pushed her away and walked back to the other side of the room, he had to get some distance between them because he knew if he didn't he'd fucking strangle her there and then and that wasn't his intention.

"O.K, we'll agree to disagree on that shall we, lets talk about you instead." He knew he had to change tack to keep his cool and walk away today without committing murder

"Are you granny yet then is there another generation of Gerraty's for you to poison and mould into your own likeness?" Of course Jez knew the answer to that but he wanted to keep playing the game for a little longer let her believe that he knew nothing of Luke until the time came to show his hand.

"You know I don't see Luke you bastard you know he doesn't even know who I am never has. Cut out trying to rile me Jez and tell me what you're here for?"

"Just curiosity Linda, you have nothing to worry about, it's just when Shirley died I thought I'd like to catch up with the woman who had nearly outed her all those years ago and thank you for the life you left her with. Just to shut the chapter of the book really, move on you know closure as the yanks call it. Seeing as you disappeared without a trace I just wondered if Shirley had outlived you know, beaten you in the end but I can see that's not the case. Just the grief of a Son trying to put some ghosts to bed."

"Jez I don't believe a word of it but I have no choice do I. You've found me, I don't know how but you have, I will make it my business to find out how you did but in the meantime I don't think we have anything else to say to each other and I'd like you to leave."

"No problem, no problem at all, nice to see you live in such a nice place, have made such a nice life for yourself, no doubt I'll see you around."

"Not if I have anything to do with it Jez!"

"Well maybe you just won't have a choice Linda. Take care of the old boy in there Paulie's not the Man he used to be but why am I telling you that, I'm sure you already know don't you?" He winked as he made his way into the conservatory strolled up to Rory and lifted his hand into his so that he could shake it. Rory's eyes widen with fear and shock but Jez gently replaced his hand onto his lap and bent down beside him whispering in his ear that he intended to sort out Linda once and for all that he should just bide his time, and keep smiling. As he turned he saw the nurse properly for the first time and as their eyes locked he realised that she was just as cruel as Linda herself. No compassion no warmth no care came from those eyes and it made her shiver to think this woman was charged with the care of this mans every need. She wasn't a nurse she was a harridan and didn't this poor bastard already have enough to deal with his heart sank for the poor sod. He walked back into the kitchen straight past Linda without another word until he reached the door and as he did he turned slowly and said

"Oh, I almost forgot Toby sends his love!" Again Jez lamented the absence of a camera as Linda's face completely crumpled her eyes shooting from side to side in panic, her lip quivering trying to keep her voice steady she held his gaze and said

"Jez if you mean Luke then I hope that isn't a threat, you know I will tear you limb from limb if you touch that Man, I will go down for a fifteen stretch because you will not escape me. I will hunt you down as true is God's my judge you lay one finger on him and you had better start saying your prayers. It still stands Jez, you want me, then you try and take me, you hurt Luke and you are fighting us both but at the moment he has nothing to do with this battle."

"Linda as far as I am concerned this is no battle, there will never be a battle all there is revenge and that will be mine." Jez turned and walked out of the door leaving Janelle shaking with anger and fear.

Chapter 26

"Get up you cunt, get up and get out, I ask you to do one thing for me you cunt and you cant I want you out now" Paulie was trying hard to come round trying to pull himself together but his head felt like cotton wool his mouth was dry his eyes felt like they had been washed in sand and to crown it all this silly cow was shrieking like a banshee and sending vibrations through the whole of his fucking body. He was well aware that he drank too much but he hadn't done too badly yesterday he would never have drank enough to let Janelle down and besides he had some hangovers from hell before and this wasn't like any of them. Neither of them were aware of the nice little stash of Rohypnol Jez had confiscated from one of the minders he employed at the agency to look after the girls when they were on a location shoot had made it's way into Paulie's drink and Janelle was definitely in no mood to listen to Paulie's excuses, she was not only spitting feathers she was choking on the whole fucking bird.

"Jan please, please stop fucking shouting my head is splitting my ears are bleeding with all that fucking racket will you just shut the fuck up woman.!" Janelle like this frightened Paulie, he had seen her in a fist fight often enough if he had watched smashing plates pulling the house apart but an unhinged Janelle having a hissy fit he had not seen before and he didn't like it, it frightened him shitless. There was only one reason she could be like this, what had that bastard done to bring this on? What had gone down while his head was God knows where? He just needed to pull it all together and get himself moving.

"Water Janelle I need water then let me think, let me get sorted I haven't got a fucking clue what's happening here so just calm down and tell me what's been going on.?"

"What's been going on Paulie is Jez fucking Watson has been in my house talking to my Husband and threatening my Son while you were so out of it you didn't even know what day it was. Some friend some protector you turned out to be, you're a joke Paulie Santini a fucking joke your past it, he took you for a right mug and you let him, you couldn't handle your drink as usual and you let him walk all over me." Janelle was pacing up and down each word being thrown out of her mouth with the velocity of a bullet dipped in poison her hatred for him at this moment was so deep. "I can't believe you've done this to me Paulie, you of all people why did you let him bring you here why couldn't you stay sober for one afternoon."

"Janelle enough. Listen to me yeah I had a drink, a few scotches nothing I couldn't handle and what I have now is not a hangover, he fucking drugged me I swear to it."

"Fuck making excuses Paulie you've lost it"

"Janelle I wont tell you again I did not drink that much. Now if you are going to carry on shouting, if you are not going to believe a word I tell you then I'm gone. I feel too fucking rough to listen to you howling and unless you tell me properly what has happened I'm off to bed and you can handle it yourself, have you got that woman because I mean every fucking word of it." He was pleased to see that the threat of him leaving had calmed her down a little and she was now sitting opposite him on the sofa with her head between her hands shaking like a leaf.

"Paulie he is after Luke, I don't know what he intends to do but he told me Toby sent his love. How does he know Luke, I haven't known where Luke was for the last two years how come Jez has that little nugget."

"He probably doesn't Janelle, he is probably just bluffing why would he know him, they don't move in the same circles he's just winding you up. We all knew he had been renamed Toby he's just making you rise to it making you sweat."

"No Paulie, he meant it alright I could see it in his eyes, he's out for revenge he told me that and I don't even know where my boy is this time to be able to protect him."

"Janelle he is not a boy anymore he's a grown man and for all you know well able to handle Jez Watson you have to stop thinking about him as your baby and accept that he can look after himself."

"No not in this, it isn't even his problem this is all because of me, I can't let him suffer because of what I have done. I offered myself on a plate to Jez, told him I would fight my battle with him but he made sure this was one battle that wasn't going to be confined to me and him he wants my boy" Janelle was getting hysterical again and Paulie was still struggling to clear his head. He left her for a second and went out to the fridge to grab some water. The scotch that Janelle had not managed to finish after Jez had left was sitting on the side and he greedily swigged it down after a few gulps of the water. Paulie had a feeling he was going to need a lot more scotch to get through this little lot in fact, perhaps he should find out about buying a distillery, he was sure it would be a lot cheaper. He refilled the glass and took it into Janelle, she put out her hand to take the glass but it just wouldn't stop shaking. Paulie slid onto the sofa behind her so that he could put his arms around her and hold the glass up to her lips. She was cold, so cold she felt like marble he was clutching onto her trying to radiate some of his own body heat into her and bring her back to life. He felt she was standing on the brink of death and it frightened him. They were both too old for this, they should both have settled down long ago and made new lives, all this shit was a young mans game and he wasn't sure how much more Janelle could take. He continued to comfort her and talk to her softly about what they would do next, how they would find Luke and one way or another get him to safety when the nurse knocked on the door to report her departure. Rory was safely in bed and she would return at seven the next day. They both managed to bid her goodnight without either of them actually turning to face her. For some reason they both felt that if they moved apart something terrible would happen, that after all these years their fates were sealed together and they had to stick together because Jez Watson was threatening the whole house of cards that they had built their lives on.

Neither of them was sure how long they stayed like that but once dark had fallen Paulie pulled himself away to shut the curtains and light the fire. It may have been summer but the evenings were getting very cold and because they were both in shock and fear they felt much colder. Paulie asked Janelle if she wanted to eat but she refused, he needed to eat himself, he still felt like shit and if he was going to be any good to her at all he would have to keep his strength up he decided to call for Chinese it had always been Janelle's favourite and it might actually tempt her to eat something if she smelt it. She too would need all her strength and courage if they were going to beat Jez, he had always been a nasty bit of work but he had been out of it all for so long, they had all almost forgotten him had imagined he's let bygones be bygones but if truth be known they all knew really that he wouldn't be able to let that happen. It would be some nice piece of work that had watched his Mother defiled like that and could walk away and forget it forever and that was what worried Paulie more than anything, with justification like that he knew that anything would go. No holding back, no holds barred it would be Jez's last chance for revenge win or lose live or die and he would stop at nothing to attain his goal. Whilst Paulie was prowling the house waiting for the food and Janelle had managed to fall into a fitful doze on the sofa he looked in on Rory in his specially adapted bedroom and felt the familiar stab of guilt that he always felt when he saw this man. Paulie didn't regret much and he couldn't say it was true regret that he felt for this poor bastard lying there as helpless a child but he did feel something. Something stirred in Paulie every time he looked at this man, yes he'd been stupid he'd been wrong to go over the side and betray Janelle but let's face. It, what man wouldn't if he thought he could get away with it and Janelle was a lot older than him. He was sure Rory knew nothing of her past but still she may kid herself that she was as good as a thirty year old but she wasn't, she was delusional, she was like most ex pros and couldn't hide all the effects of the job however much money you threw at it. Rory was only human and he had put him in this condition and to make it worse Janelle would make him watch when they were shagging, she would make a huge show of it blow him off fuck in every position possible do everything she could to tease him whilst he was stuck useless in that wheelchair but the tragic thing was he could still get a hard on and that was what turned Janelle on, watching him suffer that indignity whilst she was fucking the life out of him, Paulie Santini the man who had put him in the wheelchair in the first place and Janelle made sure he knew it. Paulie's disgust was with himself though because he allowed her to do it, he took part he enjoyed the sex and the excitement of Rory watching and that was what was worse to him they were both as sick as each other and because of that he knew their lives would always be entwined always moulded together by perversion and hate and that made him despise himself more than anything. At least Jez had led part of his life decently and at least Jez had the balls to go after what he felt was right for his Mothers memory whatever it cost him. In Paulie's mind Jez was becoming a fucking legend someone he didn't want to compare himself with because he knew there was no contest and he felt ashamed.

Chapter 27

Jez was walking on air. He knew Janelle was rattled and he liked to see her sweat. He had left her perfect home and walked to the end of the street where he waited for the cab he had called on his mobile. The people round here were definitely seriously minted, the houses must be worth well over a couple of mill and every drive was stuffed with the latest top of the range motors. Linda had definitely come a long long way over the last few years, if only her neighbours knew that they had one of the most violent notorious London tarts in their midst. He was sure they wouldn't be too chuffed, perhaps he should take out an ad in the local paper shock them all and cause her a little bit of humiliation, but no that wasn't Jez's style and he already had his plans set for Linda Gerraty. It was a shame it would have to hurt Lou, a shame that she would have to watch Toby's demise but that was tough she shouldn't be fucking the bloke behind her Husbands back anyway so she deserved all she got. After meeting Linda again today he knew he was right, she hadn't changed she never would she could still see no wrong in what she had done to his Mother, still felt no regret or remorse for taking away another Woman's life. Linda Gerraty was totally devoid of human feeling or compassion and now so was he for her. He had worried that he had began to soften with age but no, that was just something he was trying to convince himself of. Jez was ready to put all the old ghosts to rest and to do that he had no choice but to kill Toby, to take him away from that piece of scum for good, to succeed where Shirley and Tony had failed and he intended to do it soon before his nerve went. He needed to get some info from Lou, find out when and where they met. He knew it had to be a Hotel room or Toby's, Lou wasn't callous enough to take him home to Wayne's bed he was sure of that. He had made it a point lately to get closer to Lou and Toby even though it made his stomach churn, Wayne worked shifts, Toby didn't work at all and Lou was a teacher so she had plenty of time and opportunity to indulge in her extra marital.

The cab arrived and Jez was on his way home when he decided to change his mind and get the cabbie to call into the office first. The place was deserted, most of the girls on the books had jobs on today and he'd sent Terry one of the minders with Lucy as she was on a shoot with a notorious groper and she'd been nervous about going alone. Pandora was hardly seen here these days he spoke to her on the phone at least four times a week and kept her up to date on the agency business but she didn't really have much interest anymore, as long as she got her money at the end of the month she was happy. Pandora trusted Jez implicitly and he would never do her over, what would be the point? He had everything he needed, earned a bloody good wage and enjoyed his job and he had always stuck to the rule of don't shit on your own doorstep. Jez wasn't fool enough to upset the apple cart and besides he liked Pandora, he liked her a lot and saw her as a true friend. He went to the safe and rummages around at the back until he found the gun, it had been there since he started at the agency. Old habits die hard and although he was straight now you never knew what was around the corner and he believed in being prepared. Jez moved to the other side of the office and opened the draw on the left hand side of the desk where the spare bullets where kept hidden away at the back, he was hoping he wouldn't need them but he wasn't about to take any chances. He knew he would only get one pop at this and he had to do it properly so he wanted no slip ups. Jez shoved it all into his pocket and jumped back into the waiting cab to head home. The driver was still chattering away about nothing in particular when they pulled up outside his home, he paid him well and got rid of him as soon as possible, he was starting to get on his nerves with all his incessant nagging, he was like an old Woman man. Jez needed peace and quiet a bit of meditation and reflection would keep him focused.

Jez entered his own home almost warily for the first time in fifteen years he felt he had to be on his guard, tuned to the prospect of danger from Janelle and Paulie, they both knew now he wasn't going to go away again, that he had plans and a score to settle they knew that it was all going to come down on their heads unless they sorted him first so he had to move quickly and cover his own back. The house was safe, there was no one there and no one had been there, he had left a few markers to make sure, he would have known if someone had paid a visit. Jez was well aware it wouldn't take them long to find out where he lived, he had nothing to hide when he moved in, the house was in his name, he was on the electoral role, he paid his council tax so they wouldn't have to dig too deep. Jez went into the kitchen and prepared himself a large Brandy. He didn't often drink but he definitely needed one today, he couldn't make his mind up if it was Dutch courage he needed or to celebrate his small victory over Linda Gerraty at last but he needed a good Cognac to dull the edges and calm him down. He took his drink into the sitting room, kicked off his shoes and switched on the stereo relaxing back in the comfortable armchair he closed his eyes and relived the events of the day and evaluated the information he had gained from Paulie in his drugged state. Jez hated drugs with a passion, never allowed the girls to have them on the premises and when he had found Terry with the Rohypnol he had gone ballistic. He had kicked the cunt from one end of the office to the other and would have sacked the bastard there and then had he not been the best minder Jez had ever met but he had made sure he knew he was on his last warning and he knew Jez would cut his bollocks off if he ever found him with anything like that again. Rohynol for fuck's sake who was he going to use it on? That was what worried Jez most, were the girls at risk? Who was at risk from this shit? He had had to hammer it home, had to put the fear of God in him and make sure he never even thought about using something like that again, but he had to admit it had come in very handy today. Paulie liked a drink but he could also handle it, it would have taken him forever to get him out of his box like that and get him talking let alone in to a situation where he had to be taken back to Linda's, he wasn't proud of himself but he knew none of this was going to be nice. Jez picked up the phone and called Lou, the answer machine picked up which pissed him off, that meant he was going to have to get hold of that shit Toby directly and he didn't have the patience tonight to make small talk with the smug bastard in a bid to find out their future plans. He decided he would sleep on it and start again tomorrow when his brain was fresh. He knew he should eat, he'd had nothing since before six this morning but he didn't have the energy or the appetite to make anything so he headed up to bed instead. After a quick cool shower he got into bed and almost as soon as his head hit the pillow he was gone, he was obviously more tired than he had realised and he slept like a log. Never usually one to need an alarm clock because his body woke naturally at five thirty each day he was shocked to realise it was gone eight when he woke, he'd wanted an early start today but he'd blown that now, so he decided to have another half hour and jump back in the shower to wash off the sleep. Once washed and dressed he went down to the kitchen to make some Breakfast he had a huge appetite this morning he supposed because he had eaten so little yesterday. He set about making a good sized plate of bacon, eggs, sausage tomato and mushrooms, he enjoyed cooking but he couldn't remember the last time he had cooked a Breakfast like this and when he sat down at the table with a pot of tea and two slices of bread to mop up the tomato juice he was happier than he had been for a very long time. It was like a weight was being lifted off of his shoulders with the knowledge that he could finally do something about his Mothers treatment at the hands of Linda Gerraty, the time was getting nearer which was making him happy and excited all at once.

Jez finished his food and drank the whole pot of tea in three cups. He walked into the sitting room and picked up the phone again, it was the summer holidays for Schools so Lou should be at home at this time in the morning.

"Lou it's Jez, I just wondered what you were up to today?"

"Not a lot actually have you got some work you want me to do for you?"

"Nah not at the moment I just thought you and Toby might want some lunch somewhere later"

"Toby's not around today anyway what's got into you, you don't do lunch?"

"Bored, at a loose end works sorted and doesn't need me today the weathers good so I fancied getting out"

"Well you can have me for lunch but not Toby, he's been doing some work for Pandora so he'll be too busy but I'd love to come."

Jez made the arrangements to meet at twelve thirty at the London Apprentice on the river not too far away from Lou's house, he didn't really feel like a lunch of small talk he was psyched up to get moving on Toby but he needed more information so he had no choice. Lou was sweet and good company but since she had started shagging Toby behind Wayne's back he didn't feel the same about her, he no longer trusted her but he had to use her for what she knew and what she could tell him.

Alarm bells started ringing for Jez straight away when Lou had said Toby was working for Pandora. Toby was fucking work shy he'd never done a days graft in his life so what had Pan found him to do? Lou knew what Pandora was like did she not find it suspicious that little shit was spending so much time with her very attractive, very promiscuous morally lacking friend? What was Pandora up to, she just didn't give a shit who she hurt and it was beginning to really grate on him, as if Lou's life wasn't enough of a fucking mess now Pandora was shagging her lover, he was sure of that. He'd just have to hold his tongue and see what he could find out he couldn't get involved with other peoples problems at the moment he had a fucking nough of his own. Jez paced around the house all morning not really knowing what to do with himself, he was a man not used to being idle and the lack of activity and build up of tension were fucking with his brain. He had always done his own housework, never liked the thought of a strange woman prowling his house and poking around his things when he was not there and anyway he didn't really make that much mess. After all the years of living in the shit and filth that Shirley found acceptable when he was a child he was now fastidious about keeping things clean and tidy. Jez now never left washing up in the sink, hoovered and cleaned the Bathroom and toilet daily and changed his sheets every other day but he never saw it all as a chore, it had been a part of his routine for so long, ever since he had been about ten years old and he had taken over the filthy hovel they had lived in from his Mother, he just saw it as part of his life which made him different from most men. Today Jez needed things to do, to keep him busy, he was edgier than he'd been for years and his head was starting to pound with everything that was spinning around it. He didn't like taking tablets of any form and refused to take pain killers unless he was at deaths door so he thought a walk might clear his head. It was on days like this that he wished he had a dog, he had always liked dogs and he was sure on a day like today when stress was setting in walking it would be therapeutic. He also always felt uncomfortable walking in the park without a dog, he felt people were looking at him thinking he was some sort of pervert in there to look at the kids playing, stupid but that's what this shit world had come to, no trust, paedophiles and perverts everywhere and accepted by society as a fact of life and made excuses for, if he had his way he'd hang the fucking lot of them. If anyone had the choice to decide what should happen to cunts like that when they were caught it was people like him, people that had suffered at their hands and who's lives had been tainted for their sick pleasure's never understood why people like that were given second chances, let out to do it all again and claim another victims life castration was too good for them. Fuck me he really was happy today, he couldn't help himself, he was just winding himself up more, he decided the walk wasn't working and headed home to get the car, he would need to drive over to the pub so he thought he may as well stop off at Mortlake and lay some flowers at his Mothers memorial plaque. It would be the first time he had been there since the funeral which had been some fucking sad affair with just himself and a few people from the hospice who could get the time off. He would go and sit for a while see if he could find some peace as he hoped his Mother had now, now she was no longer in pain, he'd try to put his thoughts in order and calm himself for the meet with Lou.

After Mortlake Jez went along the river through Kew and Brentford and into Isleworth, he parked his car at the other end of the stretch of river leading up to the pub and tried another walk. When he arrived it was still only eleven forty-five so he got an orange juice and found a seat in the sunshine watching the boats float majestically along the river Thames, the swans, ducks and river birds breaking the shimmer as they dived below the surface to catch the morsels and titbits that people were throwing in from the edge squawking away happily to each other when their bellies were full. Jez had always liked wildlife but had never really had enough time to observe it and as he went to school so rarely as a child his education in this subject along with many others had been gained where he could find it as an adult. He liked to read, watch documentaries keep up to date with the news but he knew there were huge gaps in his formal education and if he lived to be one hundred he would never be able to catch up on what he had missed. Watching the water and the wildlife had the effect he had been trying to achieve all morning, he felt calm and in control again by the time Lou arrived he was back to his normal self. They ordered lunch, Lou a Caesar salad and Jez steak and kidney pie chips, and peas, he could not believe how hungry he was today he hadn't eaten like this for years but today he didn't seem able to stop. Lou chattered away as usual about work, the Children she taught, Wayne and Toby. Jez always found it funny that she talked about Wayne and Toby with equal amounts of affection and yet one was a shit and the other one she was making a fool of, she didn't seem to be able to make the distinction or see that she would be killing Wayne if he got wind of what was going on behind his back. Lou clearly still loved Wayne but Toby seemed to have some sort of spell on her this made him even worse in Jez's eyes because he was just using Lou and putting her marriage in jeopardy at the same time, but Jez sat and listened to the constant praise of the man he hated because he needed to know Toby's movements.

The end of lunch couldn't come quick enough for Jez once he had found out where Toby would be in the near future, he wanted to get away and think about the information he had gleaned out of the couple of hours he had spent listening to Lou's waffle. When they kissed goodbye in the early afternoon Jez was beginning to feel like a shit himself he wasn't into using people he was too honest for that, even though he was annoyed with Lou because of her behaviour he hated himself for using her, he wasn't into hurting people he cared about especially now he was older and wiser and had left his old life behind. He had to tell himself it was all necessary and a means to an end, now he could plan his next move. He was now sure that Toby was seeing Pandora as well as Lou and he knew the Hotel Pandora often used when she was meeting her married lovers so as today Toby was meant to be working for her he wondered if they would be using the Hotel room instead of her home. He decided to make a call and see if she had booked the room; it wasn't hard to get the information as the agency used the same Hotel when they called in out of town models for shoots so they knew Jez well from his previous bookings. Jackpot, Pandora had a room booked from two the following afternoon, Lou had said Toby would be with Pandora for the next week or so, so he was pretty sure it would be Toby she was going to the Hotel with, although with that over sexed little bitch you never knew but he would have to take a chance. That meant he would be kicking his heels again until tomorrow afternoon but he had no choice, he didn't really want to do this in front of Pandora and was adamant he wouldn't do it in her house that would have been a step too far. Pandora was hard she'd get over Toby and no doubt if needed she would even provide him with an alibi but he refused to defile her home and make her feel uncomfortable there in the future. He'd just have to wait, it was going to be a long night but he had to try to relax and steady his nerves. He'd done some things in his life but he'd never killed a man before and this was his mission for tomorrow, to take from Linda her precious Son, just as she had taken from him his Mother.

Chapter 28

Jez was up early the next morning with the same ravenous appetite although unfamiliar butterflies were also inhabiting his gut. He ate another hearty breakfast and settled down to the morning papers, he had a long wait ahead of him and he needed to stay as calm and composed as possible. Jez didn't want to think too much about what he was going to do today so the sports pages were taking his mind off things and keeping him occupied. He would leave at lunchtime and make his way over to the Hotel so that he could be in the room waiting when they arrived and pick his moment. It wasn't hard to get into the room like most Hotels these days the domestic staff were Eastern European and could be bought with the show of a fiver and a winning smile, for that money some would even offer to throw in sex which always made Jez laugh. All these posh London Hotels with their rich clientele were employing cheap little scrubbers with no thought for security or privacy and wondering why juicy scandal and salacious gossip were splashed around the tabloids every Sunday. You didn't have to be fucking Einstein to work out were it was coming from but they didn't seem to make the connection, fucking idiots. He got the Croatian maid to let him in and slipped her a twenty she looked like she could do with a good meal and a bath he wouldn't touch her with a barge pole, she offered to drop her knickers there and then or give him a blow job but Jez had no desire and too much respect for himself to be bothered with her. The suite was what he had expected of Pandora two rooms and a Bathroom, top billing, no shit with a bit of class. He wandered around and the opulence of it all made him laugh. Pandora was providing all this of course for the chance to spend the afternoon with her best friend's lover and the little arsehole wouldn't be putting a penny towards it. He was little more than a whore himself and yet his Mother thought she had saved him from that life by giving him up, history had come full circle and her precious Luke was now hawking his own arse for any Woman or Man as far as he knew who could provide the lifestyle he craved. Jez checked around for somewhere to wait for the lovers and decided the balcony would be the best place to wait. He had no worries that they would go into the suite and check the security or open the balcony doors to the London afternoon pollution they would be in too much of a hurry to care about that and from what he had heard Pandora was very vocal, a bit of a shouter whilst she was at it. He knew she liked people to know she was enjoying herself but if they opened the door unexpectedly he would just have to make his move there and then, Toby was no match for his strength and he knew it.

The afternoon sun was beautiful but the fumes and noise from the traffic were stifling. As Jez got older he could appreciate the country life more and the benefits of leaving the city for a cleaner healthier life, perhaps that's what he would do, move on when all this was over and he'd had a chance to sort things out, maybe he'd sell up pack up and do a Linda Gerraty disappear off of the face of the Earth and start again. if he did do that he would make sure that he done it properly, not like that stupid bitch he'd make sure he wouldn't be found and he'd cut all ties with everything and everyone, no going back and definitely no regrets. As he stood mulling these thoughts over he heard the faint click of the entry card at the door to the suite, all his senses went into overdrive and he became acutely aware of Pandora moving around the room. Shit he had been hoping against hope that Toby would turn up first then Pan wouldn't have to witness this, he could have got it done and been away again before she had even arrived but he didn't have that sort of luck. It always had to come hard to Jez nothing was ever that easy. The gun was begging to burn a hole in his pocket and his nerve edges were starting to jangle. He could see Pandora through the voiles unpacking the lingerie and toys she had brought with her, she was obviously looking forward to a good session so that should give him plenty of time to pick his moment and make sure he got it right. The door opened whilst Pan was still unpacking and in swaggered the cocky cunt and threw himself on the bed, although they were both attractive and appealing people all Jez could see was the utter shallowness the vanity and the total disrespect for other people as they started to roll around the bed in a playful embrace. He thought worse of Pandora than Toby which surprised him, he hated Toby with a passion but lets face it he was a bloke and if a bloke can get away with it he will, if it's offered and rammed in his face the most loyal of Husbands will be tempted but Pandora, Pandora was Lou's friend and had been since their School days. Pandora was someone Lou trusted, stood by and helped whenever she could, in his eyes Pandora at this moment was more of a cunt than Toby. This was a thought that would haunt him for years to come, this last thought before he carried out the action that would set his path and change his life forever. He would analyse these last thoughts so much in the future that he almost made himself believe that what happened was deliberate and his subconscious had taken over his reasoning and judgement.

Pandora had her back to the windows the fun had now become serious and she was straddled over Toby's cock rising and falling with every thrust he pushed into her. The low groan she was emitting with every vicious jab made Jez feel sick at her pleasure in such a violent act. Toby was rough with her not caring if each thrust hurt her or caused her discomfort just trying to gain his own pleasure, his hands were on her breasts squeezing so hard Jez could see Pandora squirming with the pain but Toby carried on regardless of her agony. He pulled the gun from his pocket and unlatched the safety catch he knew his hand was trembling and he could hear his heart pumping in his ears. Many's the time he had held a gun to someone's head threatening to pull the trigger and blow their brains away, many's the time he had used one for effect against some poor sod who owed money and scared them shitless but this was different, this time he would be pulling the trigger, no if's no but's and he couldn't believe the shot of adrenaline he was experiencing because of this knowledge. he steadied the gun with his left hand while he held the gun and took aim with his right. Toby was still laying beneath Pandora and he had his eyes shut savouring the moment and letting her do all the work. Looking back it was as if it all happened in slow motion. Jez's finger began to slowly squeeze the trigger his aim just to the left of Pandora's thigh where he could see the left side of Toby's chest clearly which was his intended target, he intended to hit him straight in the heart and minimise the trauma for Pandora the observer and likelihood of him having to make a second or third shot but just as his finger had reached the point of no return Toby flipped Pandora over to the left so that he could take her from behind. It was as if Jez could actually see the bullet whizzing through the air, illogically the thought crossed his mind that he would be able to run fast enough passed the bullet to block it's path, to stop it hitting it's target to save Pandora but of course that was all bollocks, that was his mind playing tricks on him. There was no way he could stop the bullet, no way could he save Pandora and the scene was like a frozen tableau in front of his eyes. Thankfully he couldn't see Pandora's face, couldn't see the pain he had inflicted as the bullet hit her back and couldn't see the stark realisation on her face that she was going to die without a doubt as that bullet ripped through her back and lodged in her right lung expelling all the air it contained and making her body slump forward onto the pristine white cotton sheet and met her end that this was one scrape she couldn't get out of, that her time on this Earth had run out. Toby seemed stunned, he had been so intent on getting back inside her and emptying his balls which were throbbing in anticipation and getting harder and harder by the second he had not even noticed Jez standing there, he had not heard a sound or even felt the presence of an intruder he was in a total world of his own were only he and Pandora existed. He was in shock, he felt removed from the scene he knew he had indulged his passion for cocaine a few times already today but he was sure he wasn't hallucinating but none of this seemed real. Time was suspended his body wouldn't do what his brain was asking him to and he just sat back on his heels staring at the prone girl he had been shagging two minutes earlier his body ejecting the sperm he could no longer hold back and his body shaking uncontrollably as the horror at his bodies reaction and the scene in front of him sank in. He wanted to scream, he wanted to run but he didn't know which to do first. It wasn't that he had any finer feelings for Pandora because to him she was just another shag but it was the shock of what he had just witnessed and the fact the thought had just struck him that the bullet was probably meant for him. He turned slowly expecting the gun to be pointed at his head but it wasn't. Jez was on his knees, he didn't feel panic just revulsion, revulsion that he had killed a dear friend, an innocent that had been caught in a fight that wasn't even hers, a girl that had her whole life to look forward to. Jez and Toby were frozen in time, suspended staring into each others eyes neither one wanting to look back at the dead girl on the bed then all of a sudden Toby jumped into action pulling on his clothes in a frenzy of activity all the time swearing under his breath and watching Jez like a hawk for any movement he made to pick up the gun he had dropped onto the carpet, any intention to finish the job he had obviously come to do. But Jez couldn't move every cell of his brain was screaming at him to get up and finish the job he had come to do, to kill Toby, to pump his body full of bullets and have the satisfaction of watching Linda's Sons face as he died, but he couldn't do it. Jez was spent, his anger, his hatred and his sheer determination had left him and he began to sway backwards and forwards on his heels not knowing what to do next, not knowing how to make things better and go back in time knowing that his own life was now over and debating whether he was brave enough to finish it now or take the consequences of his actions.

Toby had no such doubts he wanted out of there as soon as possible and he wasn't intending to call the Police before he left. He didn't know what was going on here and his brain was too mixed up to even try to think about it he needed to get away and think about things from a distance. What was wrong with that mad bastard? Why had he done this? What did he have against him? he knew for sure he had killed Pandora by mistake, Jez loved Pan, he stood her hissy fits and tantrums with patience and kindness which was more than he had done himself there was no way the guy would have wanted to kill her he was a loyal friend. Jez had the same kind of platonic friendship with Lou, could that be the problem, was he pissed at his affairs with Lou and Pandora, could he be working for Lou's Husband? No that was stupid from what he'd heard Wayne wasn't the type of bloke to get involved with murder, he was a bit of a country yokel surely this type of shit wasn't his thing he couldn't work out what was happening but he knew he had to get out now. He began to back towards the door too frightened to take his eyes off of Jez sure that if he turned away he too would end up with a bullet in his back, he just wanted out. Toby made a run for the door, Jez was still swaying backwards and forwards and repeating the name Shirley over and over again, and who the fuck was Shirley? He reached the door and made a break for freedom leaving the horrific scene behind, he needed to think, to get away from the scene and think about what to do next, he didn't want the Police sniffing round him poking their noses into his business he'd been too heavily involved with the drugs lately to want too much scrutiny from that bunch of nosey bastards. The ample supply of money his benefactor had been supplying over the years had not only sustained his appetite for coke but allowed him to dabble in the market through a fence that was a good friend. They were touching something big, a big shipment coming in from Nicaragua and he did not need this little lot spoiling it for him. Why did he ever get involved with that bloody Woman he knew she was trouble the first time he set eyes on her but that was the attraction, always had been. Who wants to settle for nice and normal when you could have a girl like Pandora who excelled at everything sexual, never balked at what she was asked to do and what's more bloody enjoyed it. Lou's adoration was just what he needed to keep his ego buoyant but Pandora was the excitement the thrill the epitome of carnal lust and that was what he craved. If Toby had known his true roots he would have known without a doubt that these traits were inherited, this was something his Mother had most definitely passed on to him and he had embraced these inherited traits. Toby and Linda had the same appetites the same lusts and the same coldness where there should be a heart but Toby didn't know that to Toby the kinks in his personality where a mystery, he knew they weren't normal but he didn't know why he had them.

Toby was free; he felt a huge weight lift off his shoulders when he left the hotel room. He had not booked in Pandora always sorted the room and he had bypassed reception and gone straight up. He wasn't stupid enough to think there were no security cameras but he had been chatting to a little bird in the lift and thinking about it the way they were flirting together and how they had left on the same floor an observer would think they were heading to a shared room, so hopefully suspicion wouldn't fall on him. As for the room, he had hardly been through the door a second and Pandora had been ripping his clothes off he hadn't had time to touch anything, use a glass even use the toilet so he should be safe there beside they had used that same room several times before so if anything did come of it he could always use the excuse that the room had not been cleaned properly but what about his DNA on the sheets, there would defiantly be some come and saliva on the bed and maybe even on Pandora would cause him problems and what about Jez, what if Jez tried to blame it on him and exonerate himself from the crime. Shit this was getting worse. He should have turned the gun on Jez, should have just blown the cunt away and made it look like suicide but his brain had not been functioning properly. He was beginng to regain reason now and realised he shouldn't have just left; he should have cleaned things up first. Panic was beginning to set in, the realisation that he could be in real trouble seep into his cocaine ridden brain

Toby realised that he was making his way home, home to safety and to where he could think clearly and relax but all of a sudden he realised that that may not be such a good idea, if Jez pointed the finger or the Police wanted to question him home would be the first place they would go. He couldn't go to Lou's because he had never bothered to find out where she lived and he couldn't go to his friends who where waiting for the drugs shipment for obvious reasons. The filth showing up there could not only fuck the deal he could end up dead if his mate took exception to them nosing around. And he didn't really have any other friends, he'd never exactly been the most popular man in town, it looked like he would have to go to his adoptive Mother Sandra's house and beg refuge. It would stick in his throat as he had never really liked her that much and he had been avoiding her calls for months, it would mean him crawling back with his tail between his legs but he didn't really have much choice, it was the only safe house he could think of so it had to be done.

The minute Toby let himself into Sandra's house he knew she was not alone, shit. He knew his Mother would never change the locks in the hope that one day he would come back so he hadn't felt the need to ring the doorbell but now he felt apprehension. To his knowledge his Mother never had visitors, since his Fathers death Sandra had become a virtual recluse and hardly socialised at all. She was a compulsive obsessive and spent all her day making sure the house was spotless and germ free if she could she would have sealed herself in a bubble so that the outside world wouldn't contaminate her, the Doctor had said it was the shock of he husbands death but Toby felt he had also contributed to her odd behaviour. Years ago when he was little more than a teenager he had been caught up in a little problem with drugs, he never found out how his Mother was informed but he had spent most of his early teenage years travelling to the other side of London to visit dens of drugs and prostitution. All he could remember was that he had gone a bit over the top at some time and the ensuing fall out had been bedlam. He vaguely remembered being taken home one night but he didn't remember by who or what else happened that night but Sandra's affection towards him changed after that night. She seemed permantly sad and very quiet, she cleaned constantly and couldn't even look him in the eye, it was as if she felt he was dirty, that he was contaminating her house, polluting her air that was one of the reasons he left when he did. That and the discovery of a bank account in his name that had over sixty grand in with more credits set up to flow in each month. Why would he want to stay in this clean freaks house when he could have a place of his own and live the life he wanted to without her interference? But all the good times were coming back to him too, the happy childhood, the holidays the dad he loved and they were all making him feel a real dick for the amount of time he had spent away from here and from Sandra. Sandra had heard the door open and shut in the hall and was standing in front of Toby before he could blink, the relief on her face at seeing him made him feel even more of a shit and she clung onto him when he leant forward to kiss her cheek as if she were frightened he where just a dream

"Mum, sorry time just got away from me, how have you been?"

"I'm fine Toby really I am" she didn't look fine she looked washed out and tired, so much older than when he had seen her last.

"There is someone here that you might want to meet but the choice is yours Toby I want you to think about it before you say yes and it will not matter if you decide you don't want to see her but your Mother is here."

"My Mother, what do you mean, why would she be here, what's she come here for?"

"She just wants to see you Toby but I have already told her that the choice is yours, she is in here if you want to see her, and I'll go and make some tea."

Toby stood staring at the sitting room door this was another shock he couldn't face, not today after all he'd been through, he wandered upstairs to his old room. Just as he knew it would be it was just the same as the day he had left, he sat on the bed and looked around him. This was his home, this was where he had felt safe and protected, his Mum and Dad had been here to care for him and protect him but then when his Dad had gone he felt suffocated smothered by his Mother and that was what had driven him away and into his drug habit and his life mixing with the wrong people. Toby had managed over the years to convince himself that it wasn't his fault that it was Sandra's that he behaved the way he did but sitting here today he had to admit he had made himself the man he was, his greed his selfishness his contempt for other people had all come from somewhere within himself and he and Sandra didn't share the same blood, didn't come from the same gene pool so perhaps it was that Woman downstairs he had to thank for the way he had turned out. Perhaps it was her fault he was how he was, perhaps he could find someone else to blame for his personality defects or perhaps he could find a kindred spirit in her, so yes he would go downstairs and meet her and face it all head on at long last. Toby took another snort of coke, he was going to need something if he was going to get through this and he knew that running away wasn't an option left open to him anymore.

Chapter 29

Janelle sat in the lounge of the woman she had given her precious child to all those years ago and she couldn't help feeling proud. The house was beautiful, old fashioned in need of decoration and not outstanding but beautiful because it was a proper family home. The rooms were light and airy the furniture well used but loved and everywhere you looked there were pictures of Luke. Janelle realised that he had a charmed childhood family holidays, the best education and a loving warm family, the only low point had been when his Father had the heart attack and all the money or all the love in the world could not have averted that event, it had been fate. His death had been the only blight on Luke's life and Janelle was proud that she had found the courage to give him up to this life. She could not pretend that his life would not have been very different if he had stayed with her and he would have had to cope with the harsh realities of the world at a much younger age especially in the early days before she had made her money and had been forced to live from punter to punter. For once in her life she could pat herself on the back and know that she had done the right thing made the right decision all those years ago.

Janelle had come here today to warn Luke, she knew he no longer lived here but had been hoping she could get a current address from Sandra for Luke to turn up like this was a bonus she hadn't expected. Paulie was out doing the legwork trying to find out Jez's where abouts and intentions but she couldn't sit at home waiting for something to happen so she had called Sandra and asked if it would be O.K if she came around. Sandra couldn't pretend that her and Toby were close any longer because he never returned her calls or visited unless he wanted something so no way had Janelle expected to see him today. What was he doing? Why hadn't he come straight in to see her, wasn't he curious about her? She could hear Sandra clattering around in the kitchen making herself busy so she assumed Luke had gone upstairs. She wanted to run upstairs after him to throw her arms around him to tell him how much she loved him but she couldn't, she knew that would be impossible and that if she did that she would ruin everything so she had to find some patience from somewhere. Patience was not something that Janelle was known for but she knew for Luke's sake she would have to force herself to exercise some. This was all going through Janelle's head and then suddenly he was there standing in the doorway staring at her as if she were some kind of alien, she could see by the glazed look in his eyes that he had just had a hit of something and that his heart as well as his brain were racing and that he was struggling for something to say.

"Luke, I, I have come to speak to you about your safety"

"The name is Toby, I have never been known as Luke and I don't fucking intend to be now. If you had been bothered what I was called you wouldn't have given me up in the first place, the name is Toby so try not to forget it."

Janelle had been shocked at the steel in his voice, she had spent years kidding herself that he would welcome her with open arms how wrong she had been.

"What do you want?" he couldn't even look her in the eye.

"I told you I have come to warn you you're not safe, some things in my past are not as I would have liked them and I have to protect you from the consequences."

"Too late as usual Mother if you are telling me my life is in danger you are too fucking late because I already know I'm lucky to be a fucking alive so you can piss off and crawl back under whichever stone you crawled out of."

"Luke, Toby I'm sorry I want to help you I need to know you are O.K tell me what's happened please, what has he done to you?" Janelle was desolate and you could hear it in her voice which was quivering with emotion, all the dreams she had about their reunion had never been played out like this, never been so awful that she wanted the ground to open and fucking swallow her up. All the pain and guilt she had suffered for all these years were threatening to engulf her she could see the hatred in her own Sons eyes and it was killing her to look at him.

"This little bit of trouble your worried about wouldn't go by the name of Jez Watson would it? It wouldn't be that mad bastard who I have just watched pump a very good friend of mine full of bullets would it? You are some fucking piece of work you spend all this time out of my life not caring what happened to me, not knowing what was going on in my life and then you erupt back into it like a fucking volcano, no 'Hello Son, how have you been, have you had a nice life, not you, you bring someone along who wants to fucking annihilate me well thanks Mother, thank you very much nice to see you too."

"I am sorry I would have given anything for this not to have happened, I have always taken an interest in your life where do you think your little allowance comes from? Who do you think bought this house, paid for the holidays made sure you wanted for nothing, Sandra and Brian were good people but they didn't have a pot to piss in it's been me that's been looking after you for all these years and that's all I'm trying to do now keep you safe."

"The only way you can help is fuck off and leave me alone." Toby couldn't take it all in it was all too much he needed to think but his mind was so fucked up with the coke and all of today's events he couldn't think straight he couldn't even string today's events together properly let alone take in all this emotional shit as well.

"Jez is dangerous Toby I don't know how much you know about him but he knows you are my Son and by the sounds of it he had already tried to take you out once today please just listen to me and let me try to help before he finds you again

"Start talking then tell me why I have just left a woman dead in a Hotel room with a bullet in her back that was meant for me, tell me what I have done for this fucking nutter to hate me so much that he wants to wipe me off this planet and start talking now before I kick you out and never see you again as long as I live."

Sandra had been listening at the kitchen door to the conversation and she was frightened more frightened than she had ever been in her life and she didn't know what to do next. Her first instinct was to call the Police she didn't want Toby in any danger couldn't bare to lose him but Janelle had realised she would be listening and had now bought Toby into the kitchen so that she could keep an eye on her. She wanted no Police involvement and she realised that this nervous quick minded little woman would see them as their saviour and would think that the law could protect them but Janelle knew that was all bullshit, she was the only person that could sort this lot out and she wasn't going to let Sandra put them all in further danger. And blow her identity at the same time.

"If he is in that much danger what do we do now?" Sandra's voice was cracking with emotion as she tried to hold back the fear and tears.

"I want Toby to come with me, I want him to stay in a safe house until we can find and stop Jez my associate Paulie is out looking for him now and believe me when he finds him he will put a stop to all this nonsense for good." Janelle was struggling to keep her calm and to stop herself swearing, ranting and raving. Since her new respectability she had trained herself to stop using bad language and only usually cracked under pressure but today she was determined to stay civil for her Sons sake to show that she knew how to behave and that she was capable and acceptable but this little mouse of a fucking woman was getting on her nerves now. Toby was looking at her in utter amazement here she was walking back into his life demanding what she wanted to happen and expecting them all to jump to attention, she was only thirty years too late but he had the sense to realise he wasn't equipped to deal with this situation that as much as he liked to think of himself as a hard man he was totally out of his depth on this one.

"We are both coming I have seen what that mad bastard can do and I am not leaving her here."

"Fine if that's what you want but we need to go now. Jez has visited this house once before in the past, he will know that you will end up here if you are in trouble and until we can find him and get him sorted you can't come back here. Get some things and let's get going the house is in Pinner we can wait there until we hear from Paulie what's happening. Where did you leave Jez?"

Toby furnished Janelle with all the details of the murder while Sandra packed a case, he told her about Lou and their friendship with Jez before all this happened and then he told her about Pandora and his shock at watching her die and knowing the bullet was meant for him. Janelle called Paulie and explained what had happened and told him to get over to the Hotel and do whatever had to be done to clear up this mess. She wanted Jez dead and she wanted it done now, she needed to make sure her Son was safe and the quicker she knew he was the quicker she could settle down to her comfortable life and forget the past for once and for all. They all left the house together in Sandra's car, Janelle deciding it would be the safest way to travel because if Jez had already turned up and seen her car outside he may attempt to follow them to the safe house. Janelle was driving because she didn't trust the other woman to get them there in one piece, her nerves were shot and her judgement clouded, but all the time she was saying a silent prayer to keep her Luke safe. She didn't care about herself, Paulie or Sandra but she could not bare the thought that she might loose her Luke again, she would lay down her life and anyone else's who got in the way before that would happen and with that single thought in her mind she drove like a lunatic over to the house she kept for severe emergencies only and she and Paulie were the only ones that knew it even existed.

Chapter 30

Jez couldn't bring himself round, he knew he had to, he knew he had to clear his head and get moving but his brain was not getting the signal through to his body, he couldn't move a muscle he just sat staring at the blood still seeping from the wound in Pandora's back. Where the bullet had entered her body the crimson pool had spread out across the sheets as the last of her life's blood soaked into the mattress and turned into russet brown. The tears were streaming down his face but he didn't know where they had come from he was numb, totally numb and awe struck. He had loved Pandora she was probably the closest he had ever come to really loving a woman and now look what he had done to her. He contemplated turning the gun on himself but at the back of his mind he knew that he had failed his Mother, that he had not yet honoured his Mothers memory that he still had work to do so he had to pull himself back from the brink had to get his house in order before he left this Earth so he had to get his mind and body working together and decide what to do next. Very, very slowly he stood up on legs that were shaking and began to move towards the bed, it was as if he were moving in slow motion the distance between himself and the bed ahead of him like a gaping chasm. He reached Pandora and gently turned her over to see if there were any faint signs of life still lingering in her useless body but there was nothing, no movement, no flicker of recognition, no sensual smile just those vacant staring eyes and the expression of pain and fear etched on the pretty face he had loved so much and that would come back to haunt him over and over again for the rest of his life. Jez began to clean the room up moving about as if on auto pilot, his mind was clear enough to know that he didn't want Toby going to prison where he would be safe if they found evidence of him in the room he wanted him dead, he wanted no chance of Linda being able to secure a cushy life for him whilst he was banged up he wanted him gone. He wanted to take any chance of Linda ever being happy again away, no hope no release date, no cosy visits or plans for the future no light at the end of the tunnel just nothing, no future no happy endings, he didn't feel she deserved one minute of happiness one second of pleasure he wanted her to live in purgatory and he wouldn't rest until he had reached that goal. Jez's addled mind felt that he now had more reason to hate Toby another item to add to his long list of misdemeanours. If that cunt Toby had not been cheating on Lou with Pandora she wouldn't have been in that room with him she couldn't have got in the way. He wished with all his heart that bastard had never been born, he would never have had this problem to sort out if that cunt hadn't been around he would have just killed Linda outright and it would have all been over and done with but because he was here it was all going horribly wrong. Toby had to die and it had to happen soon he had no choice now Janelle, Paulie and Toby would all be on their guard and he had to finish the job, he needed to get himself sorted out and out of here as soon as possible to start again and make more plans for Linda's downfall.

After clearing up as best he could he realised he couldn't leave Pandora there alone, he couldn't walk away and leave her body for God knows who to find and prod and poke over he had to stay so he would have to start thinking of a reason that he should be the one who had found the body. He would have to say that he was meeting Pandora for a business meeting and that he had walked in on this little mess and had no clue as to what had happened but he needed to get rid of the gun first. His brain was clearing and he knew he couldn't be found with the weapon, the gun was completely untraceable so he knew he was safe there, the DNA they would find on Pandora's body would of course be Toby's and the rest of the room was clean. He finally decided to go down to the Hotel bar and get a drink chat to people, make himself seen before heading back upstairs and alerting the manager and police to his discovery that made sense, make himself as public as possible. He was sure the maid he had bribed to get into the room would say nothing she had been so grateful for the money he had given her she was unlikely to jeopardise her chances of getting another large tip if he came back again and these Eastern Europeans knew how to keep their mouths shut anyway, they'd had a lifetime of practice. Jez was sure he would be safe, he wasn't afraid of being caught he wasn't afraid of prison and he felt he deserved everything he had coming to him, he would take it all but not just yet not whilst he still had Linda to deal with.

After about an hour of small talk with the barmaid and a yank who had made it his business to move next to him at the bar and yak on about st Paul's Cathedral Jez made it plain he had to leave for a meeting his partner had arranged in the room upstairs, he had already made sure his audience knew he was in the modelling business and the times he had arrived and was expected upstairs so that if questioned by the police at a later date they would be clear as to when he was in the bar. He made his way back up to the room with a feeling of dread in the pit of his stomach. He knew exactly what he would find but he didn't know how he would react to walking in and seeing her there again, having to look at that face, hoping against hope that rigor mortis hadn't set in and made her look even more accusing and ghostly than he had last time he saw her. He opened the door and entered the room; his reaction was not as he had expected he hurtled past her prone body into the bathroom and vomited into the sink and kept on vomiting time and time again his stomach retching his gut expelling all the food and drink he had consumed today. He sat on the side of the bath and began to cry like a baby, how could he live like this? What was he going to do next? He let it all come out all the hatred, all the pain and all the guilt and then he pulled himself together, composed himself enough to go back into the bedroom and called the police, all the time keeping his eye's averted from the body. Next he called reception and the manager was in the room within a matter of seconds, the police not too far behind him, then everything was taken out of Jez's hands as he knew it would be and although he was questioned he was allowed to go home and told he would be needed at the station the following day. He wasn't a suspect and they could see he was in a state of shock; they really wanted him as far away as possible in case he freaked and disturbed the murder scene and vital evidence. A policewoman took him home and that was when it really hit him, he didn't have anyone anymore to call. There was no one in this World who could give a shit if he lived or died, Pandora had been his only true friend, his Mother as useless as she was had still belonged to him had still been blood but now there was no one no one at all to tell except Lou. Lou would need to be told but she would need support and understanding herself after all she had known Pandora almost all her life he had only known her a few years perhaps if he focused on Lou's needs he would feel calmer himself perhaps if he could help her his guilt would feel less and he'd be able to think straight. He got rid of the PC and headed over to Lou's. the police would inform Pandora's family but he wanted to be the one to tell Lou, he felt it would do them both good if they grieved together.

Wayne opened the door, thank heaven for small mercies. He liked this man and he was solid and dependable that would not only help Lou but he himself needed a steady influence, a strong hand to take over in case he cracked under the pressure. Wayne saw something was wrong as soon as he opened the door and ushered Jez into the house.
"Wayne I have some bad news is Lou in?"

"She's just taken the dog out, let me get you a drink I take it Pandora's in some shit or other?"

"Wayne Pandora's dead, she's fucking dead and I have to tell Lou"

The colour drained from Wayne's face as he took in this information "No, no way how did that happen Lou was speaking to her this morning, was it her car or something? Did she have a car accident?"

"No Wayne she was murdered murdered in a Hotel in Kensington this afternoon." Wayne handed Jez a large glass of brandy his hand shaking not with finer feelings for Pandora he had always found her a bit of a pain in the arse, but for his wife, poor Lou she had loved Pandora they were like sisters she would be devastated and he hated to see his wife hurt.

"Who did it Jez how did it happen was it a client?"

"Shot, she was fucking shot I found her in a pool of blood when I went to meet her, found her Wayne I cant stop seeing her face, I found her" Hs voice kept fading as he was trying to relay the story the emotion was becoming too much for him again, he was on his feet pacing the room mumbling under his breath swearing revenge but Wayne couldn't work out who he was blaming for this it was all too confusing.

"Look Jez I think I'll go and find Lou you stay here and try to calm down a bit, she'll be over the field at the back so I won't be a few minutes. I don't want her to see you like this mate she's gonna be upset enough as it is just have your drink and try to hold things together for Lou's sake please." Wayne left and headed over to where he and Lou often walked the dog in a state of shock he couldn't believe that Pandora was actually dead, he'd had his problems with her but for Gods sake this was beyond belief and Jez, he knew they were friends but his reaction was weird, he couldn't wait to get away from the bloke he didn't really know him that well but seeing him like that was frightening him. He could see Lou in the distance and his heart sank. He had the job of telling her, her best friend was dead but worse than that was that she had been murdered. Lou had always had her reservations about the decoy agency but Pandora wouldn't listen, he'd been furious himself when he had found out Lou had been on a couple of jobs and they'd argued bitterly until she'd agreed never to go again, fucking hell that could have been Lou lying dead in that bed. Thank God she was safe thank God he still had her here today.

Lou looked across and waved at Wayne thinking he had just decided that he needed a walk but the smile froze on her face when she saw his expression. She immediately thought of her family and thought something had happened at home but Wayne quickly reassured her that her family were fine. When he told her that Pandora was dead she almost passed out, her knees buckled underneath her and he was just in time to catch her before she fell to the ground. Bailey was back at his mistress's side like a shot wanting to know what was wrong yapping and drawing attention from the other dog walkers as Lou lay on the ground sobbing, Wayne trying to comfort her. A couple of old ladies came to see if they could help but when Wayne explained that her friend had died they were at a loss to know what to do other than give a few words of comfort and wish her the best. Wayne managed to get her up put Bailey back on the lead and steer them back to where Jez was waiting in a much calmer alcohol induced haze having helped himself to some more brandy to help block out the images rolling around his head. Lou fell into his arms, sobs wracking her whole body, they clung onto each other sharing their grief and despair, Wayne felt blocked out from this outpouring and decided to retreat into the kitchen and wait until things were a little less fractious. The phone rang and he went to answer it knowing it would be Pandora's Mother, knowing that she would be asking Lou for her help because she would never cope on her own and Lou was Pandora's closest friend. Wayne was getting a bit sick of his Wife always being the one called on for help, she seemed to be needed by everyone else and no one took into account that sometimes she didn't need other peoples problems, they didn't need other peoples problems, he wanted them to be left alone to have a family and live the life he had always wanted but at the moment there was no chance of that happening.

Pandora's Mother was distraught and wanted Lou's help just as Wayne had expected but he found it a bit laughable as Carrie and Pan had never been close they didn't even seem to like each other much but now she was acting as if her world had fallen apart. From what Wayne had always understood Carrie had always been more interested in her next shag rather than her children's welfare so it was a bit too late for all this loving affection now. After speaking to Carrie Lou confirmed that she had been asked to help with funeral arrangements and that she needed some support after the death of her daughter which didn't surprise Wayne in the least. Lou had been everything to Pandora but everyone seemed to be cashing in on her pain and Wayne didn't like it but there was nothing he could do, Lou would do what was asked of her and he would have to respect her wishes and take a back seat. Jez by now was in a kind of catatonic state, he couldn't string his words together, his breathing was rapid and his eyes were unblinking, there was no way he could go home and be on his own. It was decided that he should stay in the spare room so Wayne went off to make up the bed whilst Lou held his hand and tried to comfort him the best she could. It was going to be a long night and one Wayne would rather not be part of. Carrie was travelling up on the train first thing tomorrow but he wished she were already here with her supply of pills and potions at least then they could have given Jez some sleeping tablets and given him some rest but they had never needed to keep anything like that in the house so they would just have to weather the storm.

Chapter 31

Morning came and although it should have been a lovely summers day as usual the heavens had different ideas and it was pissing it down no one had much sleep especially Wayne who had been kept awake by Jez's constant crying and moaning from the room next door. Lou had eventually cried herself to sleep and was so exhausted her night had ended up quite peaceful but Jez had too much on his mind to get any rest. Wayne padded downstairs to get the kettle on and flicked through the Yellow pages looking for funeral directors whilst he was waiting for it to boil. He was trying to help but the thought hadn't occurred to him that Pans body would not be released to them yet, there would have to be a post mortem and the enquiry into her death would need to be well under way before they would give her back. Lou came up behind him and on seeing what he was doing explained the practicalities, he put the book away and sat down with her at the breakfast table. The doorbell rang and Lou jumped up to open it to Carrie whilst Wayne returned to the kettle to finish the tea and add another cup for Pans Mother. Carrie walked in looking as bright as a button none of the previous evenings hysterics having left much of a mark on her face which Wayne thought odd, most Women would look dog rough if their Daughter had just been murdered but not this hard faced uncaring bitch. She plonked herself down in Wayne's seat and started to pick Lou's brains about the events leading up to Pandora's death but Lou couldn't give her anymore details. She told Carrie that their friend and Lou's business partner Jez had been the one to find Pan's body but that was all the details she knew as yet. At the mention of Jez's name Carrie turned an odd shade of grey and began to question Lou about him. Lou told her a bit about the relationship and that she would meet him soon enough as he was sleeping upstairs and Carrie suddenly went ballistic.

"Jez, Jez Watson is sleeping upstairs and was a friend of my Daughter, what sort of friend?" Carrie was suddenly shouting at the top of her voice.

"Carrie what's wrong, do you know him, they were just friends, just good friends and partners did Pan ever bring him to meet you?"

"I knew Jez Watson a very long time ago, I used to work with him before I was married I don't believe he knew my Daughter, Lou were they fucking each other please tell me honestly was there ever anything between them?"

"Not that I know of Carrie what's wrong? Why are you being like this over their friendship Jez is a very nice Man and he was always good to Pandora, he adored her he looked after her what's the problem?"

Wayne observing from the other side of the room thought he might have sussed out what was wrong. Pan had never made any secret of the fact that her Mother was an old slapper and he was beginning to get the uncomfortable feeling that perhaps the Man she had always called Dad wasn't actually her Father but Lou was being a bit thick here and was a bit slow to realise what was going to hit her next.

"Louise Jez Watson was Pandora's Father he wasn't aware she existed and Pan always thought that Brian was her Dad, which of course he was as he bought her up but I had her before I ever met him. Jez and Pandora had been close for ages he helped her run the agency and was a good friend but she never said anything had ever happened between them but you know Pandora she got around a bit and her second hobby was sex, her first being money" Lou didn't mean this in any derogatory way it had always been a joke between them and Lou would always think fondly of that saying now.

"Lou get him for me, I need to find out I need to know if he's been shagging his own Daughter." Carrie's voice was harsh and clipped.

"Carrie, if anything like that did go on it's not going to be his fault or her's for that matter if you never bothered to tell her the truth. If this has happened Carrie I will never forgive you I swear to God. You make me sick you should have told her, should have been sure there was no chance of something like this happening you should have been honest with her you selfish bitch."

Wayne was shocked he had never seen Lou so angry but she was spitting feathers and she was right, it was no good Carrie getting all pious and high and mighty when if this sickening union had occurred it would be all her fault. He offered to go and get Jez he didn't like to see Lou in this mood and the idea of Father and Daughter together in bed was beginning to make him feel sick.

Jez was awake but staring into space when Wayne entered his room calm but somehow frightened, he wondered if Jez had heard the conversation going on downstairs or was he still in some form of shock from last night.

"Jez mate are you ready to get up I've got the kettle on and Pans Mum is downstairs waiting to talk to you."

"Why does she want to talk to me?" he replied in a dry cracked voice"' I can't tell her anything else what does she want me for?"

Wayne was not willing to be the one to break the news of his instant Fatherhood but he felt he ought to warn him that a face from the past was downstairs sitting at his kitchen table so he told him that he thought they might have met before a long time ago. That when Lou had mentioned he was the one to have found the body Carrie had remembered his name from when she worked the London club circuit and Jez seemed happy enough with this explanation although Wayne was not actually sure how much of it he had been listening to but he felt he had done his duty none the less. Wayne lent him some fresh clothes and some shaving gear and left him to shower and freshen up feeling sorry for the poor bastard on all counts as he went downstairs. Not only did he have the death of Pandora on his mind he was now about to find out she was actually his Daughter and he still had to face this old witch of a Woman that was going to make his day and his life even worse. He wouldn't be in Jez's shoes today for anything.

The conversation was still heated and had not moved on from Pandora's parentage when he got back to the kitchen but he told them both to be quiet and give Jez a chance to get himself together before they sprang the fact on him that he had found his own Daughters murdered body less than twenty –four hours ago, a Daughter he didn't know he even had. This was all getting too surreal for him why did people make their lives so difficult, why could they not just live normal lives without all this shit being thrown around everywhere he just couldn't understand it himself. Jez entered the room and recognised Carrie straight away. She had been one of the old toms that had hung around the clubs in the early eighties. He couldn't say he was best pleased to see her she had been a right old dog giving out cut price blow jobs to drunken punters and knee tremblers down the side alley for the price of a drink, to his shame he realised she was one of the brasses Linda had made him try out when she first came for a job and no one else was around, he was gutted that this piece of shit had been his beloved Pandora's Mother he didn't want her memory sullied by this knowledge. Carrie rose and went towards him to shake his hand but Jez remained still making no move to return her greeting.

"It's been a long time Jez I didn't know you knew Pandora!"

"We were good friends I worked with her and I'll miss her but I had no idea you were her Mother."

"Was there ever anything else between you?"

"No Carrie there wasn't I respected her too much I never laid a hand on her but what business is it of yours anyway, you could hardly take the moral high ground with your history could you so if I were you I'd keep my beak out of things that don't concern you I knew Pan never got on with her Mother and now I know that Mother was you I am not surprised so why don't you crawl back to wherever you came from and leave the people who cared about Pandora to give her a decent send off." Lou and Wayne were both shocked in to silence and looked at each other with horror. They knew Jez was grieving but they had no idea he could be so cruel and hard hearted. This was a side of Jez that neither knew existed and they wanted this confrontation to stop now but didn't know how to end it.

"Sorry Jez but it is my business not only was Pandora my Daughter she was also yours so if I were you I'd stop throwing shit and look in my own back yard and see if I had anything to be ashamed of first. I have a right to know what happened to my Daughter and how she lived her life and if she was shagging her own Father I would like to know that too for my own piece of mind and sanity." Jez looked like he was about to pass out, Wayne moved in fast to steady his weight all the anger seemed to have gone out of him, all the malice and spit disappeared and he seemed to crumple in Wayne's arms.

"Your lying you bitch you fucking bitch why are you saying this you can't have known who her Father was you were on the bash taking everything that was going it could have been anyone you can't know for sure she was mine."

"Oh but I do Jez, I was always careful you see never made mistakes and if you remember after my little interview I never worked for six weeks I was knocked up in hospital with pneumonia so I know exactly who her Father was I just didn't want to admit it not to myself and not to Pandora. Why would I want to tell her that her real Father was a creepy little lap dog to a notorious London Madame, why would I want her to have anything to do with a cunt like you?"

Things were getting worse for Jez he felt like his heart was going to jump out of his chest he realised he was hyperventilating and Wayne grabbed a paper bag from the kitchen drawer in an attempt to calm him down. The three of them were struggling to understand Jez's reaction to the knowledge that he was Pandora's Father but the truth was the fact that he had just been informed he had killed his own Daughter was what was causing his anguish and he couldn't pull himself together enough to hide his emotions. Jez was having a nervous breakdown and he knew it the shaking was getting worse and he lurched over the sink to lose his guts for the second time in twenty- four hours his whole world was falling apart and he just wanted to die. He had killed his own Daughter, it had been bad enough when he had realised that he had loved that woman but now he knew she was his own blood, his only living relative, his only child it was too much for him to cope with.

Wayne took the decision to call the ambulance, no one seemed to be able to think clearly and he was seriously worried that Jez was going to croak on his kitchen floor he just couldn't get his breath and his lips were turning blue, Pandora seemed the only word his brain and mouth could form and his babbling was becoming frightening. He made the call and watched Jez carefully for any deterioration the controller had told him to just let Jez keep talking but to try and help him control his breathing by breathing with him and trying to keep him calm. Lou and Carrie were no help at all and stood by horror struck at the way Jez was behaving, Wayne was beginning to get seriously worried that he was going to end up with more than one casualty on his hands because these two seemed to be going into shock as well so he asked Carrie to go out and wave the ambulance down when it came into the street and Lou to go take the dog into the lounge as he was getting upset and running around trying to get attention. Thankfully they did as they were told and he could hear the siren in the distance he just wanted the trained help to get in and sort this out he was way out of his depth and trying to hold it all together was shattering his nerves. The two blokes that arrived were calm and authorative and took over straight away thanking Wayne for his help. They gave Jez a sedative injection to calm him down and sat talking quietly to him whilst the drug took effect; it was during this lull before the storm that the bombshell dropped. The ambulance Man had been asking Jez why this had happened, what had tipped him over the edge when he suddenly blurted out that he had killed his own Daughter, for a second no one believed him and thought he was delusional but suddenly the information clicked in Carries brain and she flew at him clawing his face, pulling his hair spitting and scratching before anyone had time to grab her and stop her harming this pathetic creature who was in mental torment. Jez sat in stupefied silence making no attempt to protect himself or stop the attack the blood running down his face mixing with the tears, snot and dribble seeping from the side of his mouth as his lips were numbing as the sedative began to work. Carrie was like a wild animal her screams blood curdling any feminine frailty gone her intention to beat him to a pulp and rip his heart from his body the way he had hers by killing her Daughter. Everything seemed to speed up one of the Paramedics already on the radio asking for Police assistance, Wayne wondered if this was because of Jez's confession or for help to restrain Carrie, he had quickly come to his senses and had her pinned with the whole of his body weight in the chair opposite Jez and praying that help would arrive soon, he wasn't sure how long he could keep her there and she was showing no signs of calming down. Wayne needed to be with his wife, Lou was starring at Jez begging him with her eyes to say that he had lied that he didn't mean it begging for the nightmare to stop but they all knew that it wasn't going to, they had all realised that Jez was deadly serious and that his confession had explained his weird behaviour since Pandora's death. Pandora's killer had been found but Wayne and Lou were no closer to knowing why, Jez had killed Pandora and why he had not known she was his Daughter but for now they would have to wait for that explanation because the Police were arriving to accompany Jez and the ambulance crew to Hospital so that they could get permission from a Doctor to question him further. Wayne and Lou were going to be left to cope with Carrie until she had calmed down enough the be of any help to the investigation.

When Jez was pronounced fit for further questioning the whole story came out, the past was revealed and all parties were seen for what they were and what they had been. Linda,

Carrie and Shirley were exposed as the drug addicted violent prostitutes they had been back in the late seventies and early eighties their parts in the drama that had just unfolded and the fact that they had laid the basis for Jez's actions all these years later plain to see. Toby was placed at the scene of the crime by the Police investigation but as Jez had admitted the crime there were no charges to be bought against him. Jez had admitted to the crime of murder but had been assured that the charge would be reduced to manslaughter and attempted murder under diminished responsibilities because his victim was not his intended target but everyone knew because of the state of his mind he would never stand trial, he had been placed on a psychiatric ward in a Hospital for the criminally insane and like his Mother before him was so heavily sedated he didn't know what day it was let alone what he had done. Wayne was spared the humiliation of his Wife's affair with Toby because the fact that Toby had been sleeping with Lou and Pandora was never made public by the Police and Lou wanted nothing more to do with Toby after realising how lucky she was to have Wayne and how much she loved him. Lou knew she had had a lucky escape and thanked her lucky stars that she was still here, she missed Pandora with all her heart and always would but she knew she had to move forward and make the family she had always wanted with the Man she truly loved and respected, she would always regret her time with Toby and knew it would never happen again with anyone else, she was happy with her life she only wished that she had known that in the beginning and not got involved with any of this mess but she couldn't change the past all she could do was look to the future and make sure she kept everyone she loved close by because at the end of the day that had been the lesson she had needed to learn. The grass is never greener on the other side it's just an optical illusion, Lou knew now that life was what you made it and you couldn't rely completely on anyone else to make it happy for you, she just wished that Pandora had realised that before it was too late and cost her her own life.

THE END

Epilogue

Toby had not committed the murder but he had escaped all his other misdemeanours unscathed. Yet again he had proved that he was more twisted than a corkscrew and could manage to wheedle his way out of anything but what was more frightening was the fact that he was reunited with his Mother and her boyfriend Paulie he had the opportunity to return to his life of drugs crime and debauchery and his power was threefold. With Linda and Paulie's criminal contacts and financial backing the Gerraty empire had the ability to become one of the most notorious and feared organisations in the country. Luke Gerraty as he now liked to be called was determined to climb to the top of his own personal tree and make a name for himself in the drugs industry this went hand in hand with the clubs and violence his Mother had known in her youth and turned her back on to become a respectable housewife. That was set to change, for the sake of her beloved Son Linda Gerraty had decided to reappear and to reclaim her crown as London's most feared and hated Woman. Linda may be getting on a bit but she'd lost none of her evilness, none of her determination and none of her bottle, she would help her boy become what he wanted and she would make sure Paulie did too. The Gerraty's were back and God forbid anyone who thought they could take them on because one way or another Linda Gerraty was going to make her Son famous if not notorious and anyone that got in the way would soon feel the full force of her wrath. The Queen might have been dead but like the phoenix from the ashes she had risen again but this time she had bought her chick with her and his heart was blacker than hers had ever been.

ISBN 1425170269